Finn

PRAISE FOR THE WORKS OF M. MALONE

"I am now officially in love with the Alexander family."
--Smitten by Reading (Grade: A-) on One More Day

"Malone has a winner with The Alexanders series! Please keep them coming!"
--Joyfully Reviewed on One More Day

"Nicholas is perfect leading man material..."
-- 4 stars, Romance Junkies on The Things I Do for You

"Malone gives her reader a story full of smart dialogue, compelling characters, and a strong story-line. The Alexanders and their friends will draw you in and keep you coming back for more."
-- 4 stars, Romantic Reads on He's the Man

This book has angst, humor, sexy times, and love. What more could you ask for? I hope there are going to be more in this series and you can bet I will be first in line.
-- 4 $^{1/2}$ stars, S.W. & More Book Reviews on He's the Man

I traveled through this book feeling a gamut of emotions: hurt, embarrassment, despair, anger, love, joy, and happiness. In the end, I loved the story and would recommend this book to anyone looking for a happily ever after ending jam-packed with lots of steamy love and intrigue
-- 4 stars, Twin Sisters Rockin' Reviews on All I Need is You

Finn

BLUE-COLLAR BILLIONAIRES #2

M. Malone

Chapter One

Finn

Hospitals always smell like death.

To take my mind off the stinging smell of antiseptic, I look over at my mother who is propped up against the pillows of the hospital bed. Tendrils of her hair spread across the cotton like soft, spidery legs. When she notices me looking she smiles but her eyes are pinched at the corners. She's trying so hard to be brave.

I'm honestly not sure why she bothers. She's never been able to hide anything from me.

She turns her head my way. I can tell she's tired because her eyes are slightly unfocused. "Remind me when I get home that I need to refill my prescription. I keep misplacing the bottles."

"Of course, Mom. Or I can pick it up for you. You know I don't mind." I'd do anything to make this process easier for her. The chemo treatments were bad enough but due to her weak immune system, she's back in the hospital because she developed pneumonia.

She grabs my hand and gives it a squeeze. The skin on her fingers is paper-thin now. Fragile. It's hard to touch her when she seems like she might shatter into a thousand pieces at any moment. And I can't live knowing I've destroyed one more thing I love.

"I know," she answers. Her attention returns to the television hanging in the corner of the room. Mom hates talk shows but that's all she's been watching since she was admitted. That and reality programs. I think it makes her feel better to see people who voluntarily have fucked up lives.

My cell phone pings in my pocket and I reach in with one hand to silence it. There's no need to look at the display. I'm late for an appointment. And I don't care.

"I have to go but I'll be back tomorrow."

She smiles when I kiss her cheek. "You don't need to come every day, Finnigan. I know you're busy."

Although she says this every time I visit, I still give her the same scowl. "Like I said, I'll see you tomorrow. Try to get some sleep."

She's already absorbed in her program again. Someone on the screen is yelling at someone else. The tinny sound follows me as I leave her room and emerge into the cool air of the hospital corridor.

"Finn?"

2

I look up to see my older brother Tank and his girlfriend, Emma. Emma's friend, Sasha, who I've met a few times at Tank's place, stands right behind them. Tank and I clasp hands and I pull him in for a quick hug. As usual, he can't resist trying to crush my hand.

"Hey, Emma. Sasha, it's good to see you again. If I'd known you guys were coming I would have planned to stick around."

Tank motions with his head toward Emma. "Em thought a mini-spa session might cheer Mom up. So she and Sasha are going to help her do her hair and file her nails. All that girly stuff that you and I are no good for."

Tank hasn't been with Emma for long but she's become so ingrained in his life that it's hard to imagine him without her now. She's also become important to me, not just because of how much she means to my brother but because of how much she means to our mom. Mom thinks of Emma as the daughter she's never had.

"Thank you. Both of you," I make sure to include Sasha. I'm sure they both have other things they could be doing on a weeknight but I know that Sasha sings in a nightclub for a living. She'll probably have to go to work after this and would rather be relaxing instead of spending time in a hospital. I can't help sneaking in an appreciative glance at the same time. With her beautiful brown skin and big doe eyes, she's hard not to notice. Seeing her reminds me that I had planned to recommend her to a friend of mine who owns a hotel. They have live entertainment and Sasha would be perfect.

"I'll get out of the way. I'm sure Mom is sick of my company."

"Call me later tonight," Tank adds. "There's something I want to ask you."

I nod but don't meet his eyes. Tank has been after me to sit down and "talk" lately and I've been dodging him for weeks. Talking usually isn't high on either of our priority lists but he's noticed Mom's pill bottles disappearing. He thinks she's hiding them on purpose or throwing them away. I can't look him in the eye and lie to him again so it's easier to avoid him. But he can be relentless when he's worried.

As I pass the nurses station, Sandy gives me a nod. She updates me on my mom's progress every morning. It helps to know what I'm walking into before I get here. Even though I know mom tells me not to come every day, I would never leave her alone. She has always put Tank and I first. She's sacrificed and worked herself into the ground to shelter and protect us. It was only recently that I've come to understand how much she's done.

I walk out of the hospital and the humid summer air cloaks me like a wet blanket. Before my feet can even touch the asphalt, a black Bentley pulls up. Jonah West, my driver and occasional bodyguard, gets out to open the door for me.

"Mr. Marshall." His eyes meet mine before darting around, assessing the environment. As a former soldier, I appreciate his diligence. A threat can materialize at any time and in any situation.

In the back of the car I stretch out, ignoring the dull ache in my lower leg. After a few excruciating minutes, I give in to the detestable weakness and prop my leg up on the seat. The edge of my pill bottle pokes me in the chest and I have to grit my teeth to resist the urge to take it out, shake out just a few pills. I can't afford to be fuzzy right now.

I have shit I need to get done today.

My phone pings again and this time I pull it out. It's my lawyer so I unlock the screen to read the email. I already know what the message will say. Still, as I scan the contract attached to the email, my heart beats a little faster. The familiar rush of adrenaline that I used to get from tactical training and being on the ground with my unit flows through me once again.

I might be laid up like an invalid, I'm beholden to my billionaire bastard of a father, my mother is in the hospital and I'm halfway addicted to my pain pills but finally there is one thing in my life going exactly the way I planned.

A second later, I lean forward. "Change of plans, Jonah. I need to get home immediately."

* * * * *

My penthouse is an architectural marvel. I bought it as an investment with part of my inheritance from my father. He hasn't been a part of my life in years but now he's back and wants to make amends. Considering that he made his fortune while leaving my mother to struggle as a single parent, I felt no shame in accepting his guilt money.

Especially once I found out that he fathered multiple children while he was neglecting us.

5

My newfound brothers are on my mind as I cross the living room and stand at the window looking down to the traffic below. I have a standing appointment to see my youngest sibling but it'll have to wait. Cell phone in hand, I take a moment to decide if this is really what I want. Because I could always allow my lawyer to handle the details and keep my name out of it. Once she sees my face, it's another story.

I hit the button.

"Mr. Marshall. I assume you've already reviewed the contracts I sent over."

Patrick Stevens came to me highly recommended as an estate lawyer but he's been instrumental in helping me with other business matters as well. It hasn't been easy navigating in the world as a sudden millionaire but I'm trying not to fuck it up too bad.

"I did. She agreed to all the terms?"

"She did. In fact, she was happy to start right away."

The words should bring me happiness or give me satisfaction. Something. Yet, I don't feel anything.

I won't feel until I see her again.

"Excellent. As I said, I would rather Miss Blake not know anything until she shows up here tomorrow."

"I've made inquiries into buying a few of her clients already. The power of attorney you signed last week gives me the ability to move quickly if an opportunity presents itself. Are you sure this is what you want?"

"Very sure. Buy any of her clients that you can. As many of them as you can. I don't care how much it costs."

He is silent for a moment. I know he must have questions. I've spent a considerable amount of money and time on this deal for no discernible reason. Why would a wealthy man care so much about the company that handles his cleaning? Despite the fact that he must have questions, Patrick doesn't voice them. He's learned by now that I keep my reasons to myself and require only that he delivers what I want. In this case, he has done exactly what I asked.

He's delivered Marissa Blake directly into my hands.

* * * * *

An hour later, I walk into Anita's Place and take my usual seat in a booth by the window. It's even busier than the last time I was here and it smells like sugar and sin. I've got a great view of the pedestrians bustling on the sidewalk outside but even more so, a great view of the waitress.

"There's my favorite new customer."

Anita Marshall appears at my elbow. Her long braids are drawn behind her head with a jaunty blue ribbon and her full lips are stretched into a big welcoming smile. She's wearing her usual uniform of a blue dress with a frilly white apron tied around her waist. When I asked about it, she said she was going for a "retro" vibe. Then I said her apple pie was so good it should be regulated by the government as an addictive substance and that she didn't need to worry about her outfit.

We've been friends ever since.

"You're late today," Anita chides playfully. She tucks the pencil in her hand behind her ear and slides her order pad into the pocket of her apron.

"I got sidetracked. But I'm here now." For a moment, I wonder if my guilt is written all over my face. Anita is a motherly type through and through and if she had any idea what I'm planning for tomorrow, she definitely wouldn't approve. She'd probably box my ears for even thinking of it.

But apparently my treachery isn't apparent because her smile is just as warm as ever.

"You almost missed him." She glances over her shoulder just as a young man, tall with light brown skin, appears behind the counter. He's got traces of her in his expression, which is currently somewhere between annoyed and murderous, but his features are something else entirely. They are at once familiar and foreign. He reminds me so much of Tank when he looks pissed off like that.

I focus once more on Anita. "I don't know what you're talking about. I'm only here because I'm hungry. And all that apple pie in that case isn't going to eat itself." I nod toward the front counter where big, fat slices of pie sit temptingly behind the glass.

Just as I finish speaking, another waitress appears and slides a plate in front of me with a massive slice of pie. "Here's your pie, Finn."

"Everyone here knows how much you love your pie. Enjoy. We'll leave you in peace now." Anita thanks the other woman and then shoos her along when she doesn't move fast enough. I have to hide my smile. Anita figured out who I was the first time she saw me. Strangely enough, she wasn't upset either. She treats me with the same sort of casual affection that she shows her own son, including exasperation when her waitresses flirt with me.

If only my half-sibling was as welcoming.

Just as I take a huge bite, Luke drops down into the opposite side of the booth and pins me with a glare. "Why do you keep showing up here? I already told you I'm not interested."

I shrug and then shovel another warm, gooey bite in my mouth. "Interested in what? Knowing me? That's okay. I'm not here to make you realize what you're missing out on by not getting to know your brothers. That's your loss. I'm just here because your mom makes this fucking crackberry pie and I can't stay away."

He scowls. "You can get pie anywhere."

"But I can't get *this pie*, anywhere. You were raised eating like this so it's no big deal to you but let me tell you, this is amazing."

Luke pulls out his phone and starts texting, making a big show of ignoring me. I take the opportunity to study him. He's tall like I am but built stockier, like my brother Tank. He's cut his hair since the last time I saw him but I know from memory that his dark hair is thick and curly. But it's the eyes that seal the deal. He looks like us. For me, that's enough. Even though he has no interest in getting to know me, I want to know him.

I've never been very good at backing off when I want something.

Finally my enjoyment of my pie seems to cross a threshold and Luke can't keep his annoyance in silence anymore. He slams the phone down on the Formica table so hard that I'm not sure it'll even work after this. He pins me with a glare.

"I'm not just being difficult, okay? There's a lot more going on here than an old man who feels guilty. I already told Max Marshall that I don't want anything from him and I meant it. And you'd do well to stay away from him, too."

His conviction is compelling. It hadn't occurred to me that Luke was resisting for any reason other than petulance. He looks so young that it's hard to remember that he's an adult and furthermore, some kind of intellectual prodigy. He probably knows a hell of a lot more about what's going on than I do.

"My mom has cancer. Saying no wasn't an option."

His face falls. "Sorry. I didn't know that."

I shrug even though a part of me feels like my skin has shrunk down a size. It's an impossible thing, thinking about my mom in that hospital bed, so I usually don't think about it. I've gotten pretty good at compartmentalizing my thoughts. I focus on the task at hand and don't think about the whys of it all.

"There's no way you could have known that. I wasn't saying it to make you feel bad. Just stating the facts. I had to take the money but I guess you don't?"

"I have money," he concedes grudgingly.

"I know. I already know a lot about you since I had you investigated." As soon as he found out about our brothers, Tank ordered comprehensive reports on all of them. Luke was the hardest to find anything on. The kid is talented enough to hide almost everything about himself. Finding any trace of him online was a struggle.

His eyes flash and then he laughs. "You really don't give a fuck, do you?"

I swallow the last of my pie. "Usually I don't. But in this case, I was pretty happy to learn I had some little brothers. Imagine my surprise to find out the youngest one is some kind of genius. Can you blame me for being just a little bit proud?"

He sits back in his chair, seemingly stunned into silence. This is the first time I've noticed a chink in his armor and I realize that despite all his denials, maybe he wants to know his brothers, too.

"I grew up with my older brother, Tank. He's built like a monster and hits like one, too but loyal as they come. He's the one you call if you have a body you need buried and he'll show up with duct tape and trash bags. No questions asked."

Luke chuckles a little at that, so I forge on.

"Now, the two I just met are Gabe and Zack. Gabe looks a lot like us except he's something of a pretty boy. Looks like the type who was captain of the lacrosse team or some yuppie bullshit like that. Somehow, Zack is the exact opposite even though they grew up together. He's the tatted up, Mohawked, silent type. But word is, he's a genius with anything on wheels. He fixed a car for Tank's girlfriend and the thing runs so smoothly that she won't let Tank buy her a new one. Drives him crazy."

I glance over at Luke. "Then there's you. The child prodigy. We have a file on you that reads like fiction. I barely made it through high school and probably wouldn't have if I hadn't charmed the panties off some of the smartest girls in school who did my homework for me. And here you are, writing software that saves people's lives. So yeah, I'm just a little bit proud."

Luke doesn't say anything but his eyes stay on mine for a long time, like he's trying to read the truth of my words in my face. For a moment, he looks almost wistful, like he'd give anything to take me at my word. Then just like that, the look is gone and his face shuts down again.

"I've gotta go." He shoves back from the table and I watch his back until he disappears behind the counter again. Anita looks over from across the room where she's helping a boisterous family of five. She gives me a sympathetic smile.

With a sigh, I pull out my wallet and leave a twenty-dollar bill on the table. I won't be getting through to him today. But that's okay.

There's always tomorrow.

Chapter Two

Rissa

We're saved.

I look down at the contract on top of my desk. I'm not sure what angel heard my prayers, pleas and the wild sobbing into my pillow last night but it worked! This one contract to clean a pricy high-rise in Norfolk will be enough to keep my cleaning business, Maid-4-U, afloat.

"We got it?" Daphne, one of my partners, sits on the arm of my chair and peers over my shoulder. Her blue eyes widen and she lets out a shriek.

"Is that how much they're paying us? Shut the front door!"

I burst into laughter at her exuberance and for once don't even bother to try to get her to curse like a grownup. In the past six months, I've dropped enough curse words for the both of us. Like the time our electricity was shut off and Tara had to take the laptop down to the local coffee shop that has free Wi-Fi to do payroll. With the amount of money we'll pull in from this one deal, we won't have to worry about that again for a long time.

"Tara, get over here! You have to see this."

Although I shake my head, I don't say anything when my other partner, Tara Petersen, shoves me to the side.

We're not too formal around here. The three of us have been working together for a few years now, just three broke girls who managed to turn cleaning houses into a thriving business.

Tara picks up the contract and her lips move slightly as she reads it. She's the stickler for details so I know her analytical mind is searching for potential errors or pitfalls. Her brown hair is sticking up all over the place as usual and with the blue streaks she recently added she looks like a high school kid. It's funny that she's the smart one of all three of us since people usually assume that I'm in charge. If Tara wasn't so abrasive she'd be the one who negotiated with the clients instead of me.

She turns to me and then places a hand on her hip. "I can't believe you actually pulled this off. You said you'd been bidding on bigger jobs but I had no idea it was this big. How did you convince them to pay so much?"

"I wish I could say it was superior negotiation skills but I really have no idea. This company found us. They were searching for a new cleaning service and asked for a quote. I got a call a few days ago that they'd reviewed my presentation and decided to go with us."

"This is what we've been waiting for," Daphne declares. "Our luck is finally changing!"

Tara looks up from the contract. "I wouldn't get too excited just yet. Did you actually read this, Ris? They made some changes."

I snatch it back. "I read it. I mean, I sort of read it." Her pointed look makes me feel like a kid in the principal's office. "I read the original and that lawyer guy told me what changes he was making. So, that's good enough. I'm sorry. I just couldn't read through all that boring blah, blah, blah again. I fell asleep reading it the first time."

"Well, there's some weird stuff in here." Tara picks up the contract, waving it around as she makes her point. "It's super specific about what time the cleaning has to happen and it's early. It says by eight am everyday. Also, the cleaning for the owner's penthouse has to happen with him present and here's the weird part; it has to be the same maid every time. If we send a different maid, that's considered a material breach of contract. I mean, who the hell is this guy? Is it someone famous?"

I stand up, coffee cup in hand. I've always been an early bird but since I'm now required to work such late hours, coffee is a main staple in my diet. There's no way I could stay awake so long without it.

"I have no idea but I doubt it's anything that exciting. The name on the contract is some kind of company. I got the impression that most of the units are vacant."

"Maybe they just need it to be the same person so they can do a background check and be sure the person entering the owner's place is trustworthy." Even as she says it Tara doesn't look completely convinced. "Well, either way this is a huge contract for us. I'm not sure how we're going to handle this. We do have a couple of people who have asked for more overtime but we still need someone for the owner's suite."

"I guess I could do it." Daphne offered. "I usually work that time of day anyway."

Tara and I must have been wearing identical expressions of skepticism because Daphne crossed her arms and pouted. "What?"

I walk over to the counter and then sigh when I see the coffee pot is empty. "It's nothing Daphne. It's just, what if the client is there and he's a jerk?" Daphne is an absolute sweetheart but she can't handle conflict. At all. If the client is difficult, Daphne would end up in tears within ten minutes.

Tara doesn't have any problem laying it all out there. "You don't handle jerks well, Daph. He'd hurt your feelings and then I'd have to go kick some ass. So that won't work. I guess I should do it."

This time, it's Daphne and I who exchange looks. Finally I speak. "Um, Tara. If he's a jerk that means you'd have to be nice and hold your tongue every time you see him. I don't think that'll work either. I'll do it."

Tara shakes her head. "You're already handing the Johnsons in the afternoon and the Mercer account in the evenings. You'll be dead on your feet working that many hours."

"We can switch some things around. The Johnsons don't care if it's me cleaning their house or someone else. A couple of the part-time girls have been asking to go full-time anyway and now with this contract, we can finally afford to hire more help."

Tara narrows her eyes at me. "Okay but I've got my eye on you. You already look dead on your feet. I'm going to tell Gloria if you don't behave."

That makes me smile. My mom has been there since we started the business and she even worked shifts for us in the beginning. Once the business started to pick up, I made her cut her hours to only part-time. It's been the greatest gift in my life to be able to help my mother, to take some of the weight off her shoulders. She's always worked double-shifts to take care of us and for the first time in her life, she's able to take it easy. Go out with friends and not have to stress over bills. I'll do anything to keep it that way.

"Gloria is having a ball dating some gentleman she met in line at the grocery store."

Tara laughs. "Only your mom would find a date while running errands. She can make sweatpants the new sexy."

"I know. I wish I'd inherited that from her."

"Uh, you did Miss Double Ds. Duh," Tara makes a face. "You inherited her body and her work ethic. But that doesn't mean she'd want you to run yourself into the ground."

"I'll be fine. I can handle it." I stress the last word, hoping Tara gets the hint.

She knows that I've been going through some things lately but hopefully she won't say anything in front of Daphne. I don't need them both worrying about me. Working more hours won't hurt me, if anything it'll help me because I'll have less time to think. That's what I need the most right now, oblivion from thinking about the mess I've made of my life with my crappy choices.

I pick up a pen and sign the bottom of the contract with a flourish. Daphne signs next and then hands the pen to Tara. She stares at me for a long moment, then finally sighs.

"I guess we have to take a chance."

"It'll be fine, Tara. Don't worry so much."

"I don't know what you two are yapping on about. We should be celebrating. *This is a sign*. Things are finally looking up for us girls. Woo hoo!" Daphne does a little booty dance next to the desk and we all burst into laughter.

Their laughter and silliness is exactly what I need when my phone in my pocket suddenly feels as heavy as a brick. I should have never told Tara that Andrew was calling again, trying to establish contact. It was a point of shame that I'd never pressed charges against him but all I want to do is forget that time in my life. Now she's worried about me and she doesn't need to be. I'm not that person anymore.

I finally have it together and I won't let anything take this away from me.

* * * * *

The next day I arrive at the address listed on the contract and stand outside just staring up at the imposing building. On the outskirts of downtown Norfolk, it's obviously been recently renovated.

My fingers curl around the tight band of my pencil skirt. Usually I'm wearing the same basic uniform as the rest of the maids, casual clothing covered by a green and yellow Maid-4-U apron that Daphne designed for us last year. But today, I'm here to bring the signed contract to the client and see the area we'll be working in. I have to look professional. Put together.

I swallow against a wave of nerves and run my hands over my hair again. The unruly red curls tend to have a mind of their own so I've pulled them back into a low bun. I can't screw up this job. This could be the start of a whole new wave of luck for our business. Daphne is the optimist, but secretly I'm starting to agree with her that this new deal is a sign.

Our luck is finally changing.

After my moment of self-reflection, I walk into the lobby. It's not as impressive as I imagined it would be. Considering the amount of money we've been offered to clean this place, I was expecting solid gold floors and diamond encrusted door handles. But it's just a plain entryway painted builder white.

There's a man behind the counter. I nod at him and then take a seat on one of the couches in the waiting area. Mr. Stevens is supposed to meet me here and take me up so I can see the property and meet the owner. After about ten minutes, I pull out my cell phone. Where is he?

What is it with rich people? They always think everyone else should be on their timetable. It makes me think about Andrew. He'd done this type of thing often. He would rush me along but consistently show up late or not at all when I needed him. The only time he'd really shown emotion was anytime someone mentioned my relationship with Finn.

I close my eyes.

Even now years later just the thought of him is enough to bring tears to my eyes. *My sweet, Finn.* His family lived in the same trailer park and we'd shared the experience of being the trash from the wrong side of the tracks at our school. He'd been my first kiss, my first love. My first everything. Then after school he'd gone off to the army and things had never been the same.

I'm suddenly pulled from my thoughts by the sound of my name. The man behind the front desk is standing now, peering at me with interest. "Miss Blake?"

"Yes, that's me."

"Mr. Stevens just called. He told me to let you up immediately." He stands and walks to the elevator. I follow him on and then watch as he inserts a key from the massive ring in his hand. He twists it and then punches the button for the twelfth floor. I watch in surprise as he steps back out. The doors close behind me and the elevator hurtles upward.

The nerves I felt downstairs come back full force when the doors open with a ding. I step out of the elevator and into a hallway. There are doors at the end of the hallway in both directions. I let out a little sigh. It all seems a little rude, to summon me up here but not have anyone waiting to show me where to go.

I look down the hallway to my left. The door to 15B is partially open. *That must be it, then.* I walk down the hall, my feet sinking into the deep luxurious carpet. When I push open the door, it doesn't make a sound.

"Hello?"

I walk inside and then stop in awe. It's so beautiful. I never even knew that apartments like this existed in Norfolk. The ceilings are much higher than normal. I estimate that they must be at least fifteen feet high. The room I'm standing in has two large, deeply stuffed couches angled to face the windows. To my left is a beautiful gourmet kitchen with tall, cherry cabinets and gleaming stainless steel appliances. There's a hallway to the side that must lead to the bedrooms.

I'm going to be working here? As I look around in wonder, I have to ask why the owner even hired me. The place looks pristine already.

There must be some mistake. Maybe the owner just wanted to meet here so we could talk about the contract before he shows me the apartments in the building that actually need cleaning. But even still, I'm sure the other apartments in the building must be lovely, too.

"Hello? Sir?"

It hits me then that I don't even know the owner's name. Mr. Stevens has been my contact throughout this entire process and although there was a company name on the contract, I didn't even think to ask the name of the representative the company would be sending over.

"Do you like the view?"

The deep voice comes from the shadows of the hallway. Even though I just called out for someone, it startles me. And all at once, it reminds me that there's no one else here. When I agreed to this meeting, it was under the assumption that Mr. Stevens would be present as well. But now I'm alone with some man that I've never met.

A man with a voice that's both haunting and terrifying.

"I do. This is a beautiful place," I answer, hoping that he'll come out from the hallway so I can see what he looks like.

I really hope he's not creepy or some kind of jerk, the way Tara thought. But even if he is, I'll have to deal with it because we can't afford to lose this contract.

"I bought it just this year. I enjoy surrounding myself with beautiful things."

His words are strangely inappropriate yet I'm enthralled. I should be angling closer to the door so I can get the hell out of here if he does anything weird. But I can't move. There's something about his voice. The way he speaks. It's familiar and heartbreaking all at once.

"You pulled your hair back. Hair like yours should never be restrained."

Even before he steps forward, my traitorous heart skips a beat. How could I ever forget that voice, the voice that promised me that

I'd never be alone, that he'd always be there? That we'd be a team. The voice that told me I was everything before I was foolish enough to throw it all away.

"Finn?" My voice comes out as a whisper and I hate myself for the weakness.

"Rissa."

My eyes almost roll into the back of my head hearing him say it. No one has ever been able to make words into a caress the way he does, rolling the letters over his tongue like he wants to make love to every inch of me starting with my name. Against my will, memories of the pleasure I once knew at the mercy of that tongue roll through me. The things he used to do ... Heat blossoms and unfurls inside me, spreading through my limbs until I have to grab the back of the couch behind me to keep from collapsing into a heap on the floor.

"What are you doing here?"

He steps out from the shadows of the hallway and into the light and I gasp. Without a thought or care, I spring forward my arms outstretched.

"Finn? What happened to you? Are you all right?"

He's walking with a slight limp, relying heavily on the ornately carved cane in his right hand. In my shock, I don't notice the distaste on his face at least not until he takes a step back.

"I'm fine." His curt reply leaves no room for misinterpretation. Whatever happened to him isn't something he'll be sharing with me. The rejection stings but then again, considering our history, why should I have expected anything else?

"Where's Mr. Stevens? Do you work with him or something?"

Finn walks forward, passing me without comment. Then he settles himself on the couch and rests the cane against the arm next to him. "Mr. Stevens works for me. He's one of my lawyers. I had him handle procuring a cleaning service on my behalf because I simply don't have the time or desire to do it myself."

His words are so impossible that I just stand staring at the back of his head for a minute. His hair is slightly darker than it was when we were in high school, more brown than blond. But he still has the wayward piece in the back that grows in a different direction than all the rest. The sight brings it all home and makes it real. This is Finn.

And he owns this building.

"You're the client?" He doesn't acknowledge me but I know instinctively it's true. I walk around and take a seat on the couch facing him.

"He came back, Rissa."

"Who?" I'm still so shocked that he's here that I'm having trouble following the thread of the conversation.

"My father. He's back. And he's wealthy. So now I am, too."

This is huge. Growing up, we had so many conversations about our fathers. I've never met mine and Finn's took off when he was small. I know how big of a deal this is for him. But he seems strangely nonchalant about it, like it doesn't even matter. And I don't know him well enough anymore to gauge his mood.

"So, why did you hire us?" Moving the conversation back to business seems to be the safest course.

"Your business offers cleaning and home management as well, is that correct?"

"Well, yes."

"That's why I hired you. I need a cleaning service for this entire building and someone to handle organizing my space as well."

Stunned, I just stare at him. How does he even know that we do all that?

When Daphne, Tara and I first started, we envisioned a service that helped people organize their entire lives. From keeping appointments to closet reorganization to cleaning. Everything. Unfortunately in this economy most of our customers don't have the money to hire us for any extras. Most just want cleaning services and many have scaled back to only monthly cleaning. Weekly or daily clients are hard to come by.

Now here is our first client willing to pay for the full-service and it's someone that I can't deal with.

"So you hired me, even with our history?" Something about this isn't right. Why would he do that? Unless he's trying to start something again. The last time we spoke was when I ran into him randomly in town before he was deployed for the last time. I'm the one who broke things off so I wasn't expecting him to be happy to see me but he hadn't even been able to look at me then. So why would he seek me out now?

I look up and he's watching me. The same current of heat passes between us and something clenches deep and low in my belly. "You didn't bring me here thinking that we would … you know."

Finn's jaw tightens, the only outward evidence that he's disturbed.

"Why would you think I wanted that from you? Men in my position stay away from gold-diggers if at all possible. You've already proven what you're about."

The pain comes out of nowhere, like a shot in the dark. I close my eyes. He's so angry. This isn't like him, not like the Finn I knew. He always had a smile for me. Always knew just what to say to make me feel better when I was sad or tired. He understood the frustration of wanting more and not knowing how to get it. And for a time we were each other's shield against all the things that would attempt to hurt us. But then I met Andrew and everything changed.

He speaks and it's like he's reading my mind, as if my thoughts of the past have triggered his own.

"How is Andrew, by the way? I hope he's well."

His formal tone of speech just makes it clear that he's mocking me. Finn was never formal with me, or with anyone really. I have no doubt that he already knows that we're not together anymore. He looks too pleased with himself not to have that information already. I'm sure he just wants to rub my nose in it, in how spectacularly wrong I was when I made my choice.

"He's just fine."

"Of course he is. He has you, so why wouldn't he be? You two are perfect for each other."

I have to clench my hands beneath my legs to keep still. He has no idea just how deep his verbal barbs have penetrated. I'm sure he also has no idea just what a sadistic monster hides behind Andrew's perfect face. If he knew, I don't think he'd be saying these things. Finn was a jealous type but never evil. And even though he'd feel sorry if he knew the truth, I'll never tell him just how imperfect things actually were. I don't need anyone's pity. I got myself out of that situation on my own and I don't need anyone looking down on me or crying tears on my behalf.

"Anyway, I'd love to catch up but I need to show you around and give you your keys." He stands, relying heavily on the cane. When he looks up and sees me watching him, his face hardens.

"And I need to tell you exactly what I expect from you."

* * * * *

I follow behind as Finn shows me the rest of the building. The other apartments aren't as stunning as his but they're all newly renovated and spacious. *He owns all this now.* These types of apartments are the kind that we could only dream of living in as kids.

We're standing in the middle of one of the vacant units when his phone rings. He holds up a finger as he answers.

I walk away slightly to give him some privacy but I can still overhear part of the conversation. It must be someone who works for him. It's so odd to hear him talking with such authority. It's like observing a stranger except this stranger looks like my Finn. Talks like my Finn.

I have to remind myself that he's not. The boy I loved is gone. The Army took him just as surely as if he'd died overseas. And

27

anything that was left when he came back, I killed when I gave him back his ring.

"Are you listening, Marissa?"

He's watching me and I realize I've missed something he said.

"I'm sorry. This is a lot to take in. What time do you want your maid to come in the mornings?"

He tilts his head. "I expect you to be there by eight o'clock sharp, just like it says in the contract."

I'm already shaking my head. Even though I told Daphne and Tara that I would do it, that was before I knew it was him. There's no way that I can show up here everyday and be around Finn without the past crashing back in on me. I've worked so hard to move on and all of this has brought that pain dangerously close to the surface again. I'll be lucky to get out of here today without breaking down completely. But I won't let him have that victory.

"I'll be sending someone else to clean your residence. Now that I've seen the place for myself, I'll start assembling crews to handle the other floors."

Finn just looks at me, his eyes blazing. The look on his face is so potent, so intense that I actually take a few steps backward. As if I could escape him that easily.

"It has to be you. *You.*"

"The contract said that we couldn't send a different maid. I'm not here as a maid. I'm here as the owner."

"It will be you or the entire deal is void. I want you here everyday. You'll clean and decorate the place. The only area of the penthouse forbidden to you is the master bedroom."

He's being so unreasonable that I have to fight back a tide of curse words. It's like he's determined to make this as difficult as possible. Then I realize that's exactly what he's trying to do.

"If we're expected to clean the entire building then I'll be of more use directing the cleaning crews."

"It's you or no one. Think carefully, Rissa. I don't think the bank will give you any more extensions on your loan."

His casual mention of my loan just confirms what I already suspect. He knows just how precarious my financial situation is and he's using that to his advantage. I wonder if he laughed as he made the offer, knowing that I would have to take it. He probably thought it was amusing to dangle this big contract in front of me and then watch me scramble to meet all the requirements.

But I have no choice but to dance to his tune. Because he's right, if I miss any other payments the bank might call my business loan. I have too many employees counting on me to fail now.

"Fine. I'll be here tomorrow by eight."

His face doesn't change but something in his expression relaxes. He was expecting me to protest again, to fight harder. Why is this so important to him? The vibe I'm getting from him definitely isn't romantic but his insistence on keeping me close doesn't make sense otherwise.

He gives me a small smile. "Don't be late."

Then he turns and walks away, leaving me standing in the middle of a beautiful vacant apartment all alone.

Chapter Three

Finn

I've been living alone ever since I was twenty. It's been a long time since I woke up to the sound of someone in my space. My dreams are still hanging in the back of my mind so I'm not sure how much is real. I can only guess what some of the sounds translate to. Faint shuffling sounds could be her feet moving over the hardwood. Something bangs. Probably cabinets closing as she looks for cleaning supplies. I can picture her in my mind, moving around my kitchen.

The image of her from the prior day is burned onto my retinas. It's not that I didn't know what she would look like. The reports I have on her are filled with pictures. Smiling pictures, angry pictures.

Pictures of her from the society pages on the arm of the man she left me for.

None of them could have prepared me for the sight of Marissa Blake in the flesh.

I'd originally thought I'd sit out front and watch her clean but after yesterday, I find I don't have the same level of enthusiasm for this plan that I thought I would. Punishing her sounded like such a great idea before this. I wanted to bring her here and show her everything she could have had. Show her that she chose wrong and that I'm not just some loser that couldn't take care of her properly. But that was before I saw her. There's something different in her eyes now. She looks like she's been punished some by life already.

And now I just want to lie here with my eyes closed and indulge in the completely ridiculous fantasy that Rissa is in my apartment because she wants to be.

The fact that I even *want* to imagine that pisses me off so I throw the covers back and roll to the side. My leg aches like a bitch already and I haven't even gotten up yet. Pain is so exhausting. It takes everything I have some days to fight through it.

I finally sit up and manage to stand. Luckily once I'm upright the sharp pains settle into a dull ache. Hopefully a hot shower will ease it a little. At least long enough for me to get through the morning. I don't want Rissa to see me like this. Then I remember her shock and pity at seeing my cane yesterday. She's probably already glad she didn't end up with me. Andrew Carrington is a prick but at least he's whole.

There's another bang up front and I glance over at the clock. It's a little after seven. Clever thing. I can't help but be impressed. The contract specified that she was to be here by eight. It never stated that she couldn't come earlier.

I'm sure she was hoping to wake me up.

My mood darkens as I realize that Marissa is remembering the boy who loved to sleep in. The man is used to Army hours and waking at seven is considered lazing the day away. Plus, time doesn't mean the same thing when you have insomnia most nights.

By the time I emerge after my shower, everything is quiet. In a panic, I move down the hallway. The kitchen is empty and I whirl around, wanting to punch the cabinets. There's no way she finished everything and the contract specifically states that she's supposed to be here until noon.

"Finn, what are you doing?"

I turn at the sound of her voice. She's using some kind of tool to brush the cushions of the couch. Relief sweeps through me.

She didn't leave.

Then I take in the shocked look on her face. She's very deliberately looking anywhere but at me. Her cheeks slowly turn pink.

I look down at the towel around my waist. I didn't even realize that I wasn't dressed yet.

"I was coming out here to … uh, tell you that I have some laundry that needs to be done."

It's the first thing that pops into my mind and I hope she doesn't call me on the weak excuse. Why would I need to tell her that I have laundry that needs to be done? I've hired her to clean this place and laundry was in the contract. It's hardly the kind of thing that requires a warning. But she's still looking at the couch cushions as though they hold the secrets of the universe. Then she glances up at me, her eyes lingering on my bare chest before her gaze drops to where my towel knots low on my hips.

I guess I'm not the only one affected here.

Part of me wants her to come on to me, to try to use her body to get out of our arrangement so I can turn her down cold. But right behind that desire is the very real understanding that if Marissa Blake ever tries to use her body to get me to do something, I won't be the winner in that scenario. I don't have a good track record at denying her anything.

Finally she meets my eyes. "Laundry. No problem."

She's not the only one who can pretend to be unaffected. "I've also got some mail that needs to be sorted. Can you go through, pull out anything important? Shred the junk mail."

I've already gone through all the mail so I know there isn't anything in there that I don't want her to see.

She nods. "Sure. Do you want me to get the laundry from your room?"

"The master is off-limits to you," I remind her.

"Oh yeah." She bites her lip. "I'm not going to go through your things, you know."

"That's not why it's off-limits. I don't let just anyone in my

33

private space. And if you ever step foot in there, you're going to be doing a hell of a lot more than cleaning."

She stares at me so long I wonder that she doesn't see right through me. At first, she looked like she was averting her eyes out of modesty. She was always strangely bashful about nudity, something I would have thought she'd gotten over as an adult woman. But when I step closer, she looks pained, like she's trying not to flinch.

She doesn't think I'd try to force her to do something against her will, does she? Maybe that's happened before. If she's cleaning for people in their homes, she could have been in this position with a man before. A rush of anger is followed by a fierce surge of protectiveness. I want her to pay but not like this.

Never like this.

I take a step back and her sigh of relief is audible. "I'll just go get that laundry."

Before I reach the hallway, the sound of her voice calls me back.

"Finn? Why did you give me this contract? I mean, what's really going on here?"

The answer to that question is so complicated. It's more than just wanting to show her what she missed out on, more than just anger, more than just revenge. The answer contains things that even I don't want to contemplate too closely so I just settle for another question.

"Why wouldn't I want to help out an old friend?"

* * * * *

"Come talk to me while I eat my breakfast."

34

Rissa looks up from where she stands across the room. She's moved on from her vacuuming and is now using a can of something to buff and polish every surface in the room. She's only been here a few hours and the place already looks amazing.

"I'm working, Finn." There's a subtle reprimand in her voice and it's so familiar that I can't help but smile.

"You can't work and talk at the same time?" I sound petulant even to myself but I want her to talk to me.

Rissa isn't having it. She rubs vigorously at a spot on the coffee table. "It's not that easy for us poor, working folk. Not that I should expect better but considering where you come from, I guess I thought you'd get it."

There's a bit of disbelief in her voice that makes me feel a little ashamed.

"Where I come from?" I ask, pretending I don't know what she means.

"Yeah. Working class. Just like me. How is your family doing? Your mom was always really nice."

"Not so great, actually." Normally I wouldn't have even said anything. Most people who ask after my mom, I just say 'she's fine' and keep moving. But Mom always really liked Rissa. It was a weird thing as a teenage boy to have a girlfriend who fit so seamlessly into my family but it was also confirmation of what I knew the first time I kissed her. Rissa was perfect for me.

"She's in the hospital right now."

That gets her attention. She stops her buffing and looks over her shoulder at me. "I'm sorry. Claire was always so sweet. Is she going to be okay?"

"I honestly don't know. She has a particularly aggressive type of cancer. We've flown in specialists and we're trying to find something that will help her. Something that will keep it from spreading. But I honestly don't know."

She's watching me closely. Her eyes on me feel like a balm to nerves that are suddenly raw. "I really hope you find something that will help her."

"Yeah, me too."

"What about your brother? Is Tank still around?" Suddenly she pauses and leans against the couch for a moment. Her eyes close and only then do I notice the shadows beneath. I recognize the signs of exhaustion. I see them everyday in the mirror.

"Rissa?"

She opens her eyes immediately and starts moving again. "Yes?"

"Did you eat this morning?"

She shakes her head. "No, I didn't have time to stop for anything. But I ate last night when I got home. That wasn't that long ago."

I narrow my eyes at her. "How was that not that long ago? Unless you ate in the middle of the night?"

"Well, yeah. I usually get home a little after midnight and eat before I go to bed."

"Midnight? Late night partying?"

She gives me a disgusted look. "Working. Do you seriously think taking care of you is my only job?"

Due to the extensive research Patrick Stevens did on her business, I'm well aware of how many other clients she has. Not that I want her to know that. So I hadn't thought I was her only job but I had thought that once I hired her, she'd assign her previous work to someone else.

"Wait so you're cleaning my place until noon and then what, you go to another cleaning job in the evenings. Which means you get home late every night? When do you sleep?"

"Sleep is optional at this time in my life. Paying my bills isn't." Suddenly she bolts straight up. Then holds up a black thong with the tips of her gloved fingers. "Are these yours?"

Oh hell. I actually forgot I left those there for her to find. Suddenly my plans seem petty and juvenile, especially in light of what we were just talking about. But then I remember watching her walk away and into Andrew Carrington's arms.

She didn't just hurt me when she gave me my ring back. She crushed my pride by making me watch her with the guy who taunted me for being trailer trash. The guy who'd looked down on us both at one time. Before she grew up and he noticed how beautiful she was.

So I shrug, as if finding some random woman's thong in my couch is an everyday occurrence. Then I smile knowing it'll just piss her off.

"Well, in that case I won't bother saving them." She shoves them deep into the trash bag at her side and resumes looking through the cushions. She pulls out a condom wrapper and tosses it in the trash bag as well. There's no mean looks or snide remarks but I can feel her shutting down the longer the silence stretches on.

I feel the loss of the connection acutely. For a moment, it felt the way things used to feel between us. Easy. Like we could talk about anything. It's the kind of thing you take for granted until it's gone. Until you spend years having unimportant conversations with people who don't matter and remember what it was like to have someone who really heard you.

"Rissa. You should eat something. You know you get migraines when you don't eat."

She shoves something else into the trash bag. "I'm fine, Finn. You don't need to worry about me. I'm not your responsibility."

I open my mouth to say something. I'm not even sure what, but before I can get it out, the sound of the vacuum drowns out anything else I might have wanted to say.

Rissa doesn't look my way again.

* * * * *

"Hello? Finn, are you here?"

My eyes open at the sound of her voice. Confused, I turn to look at the time. After Rissa left, I went to visit Mom and then came back home to take a hot bath. My leg was aching so I took a few pain pills and let the jets in my soaker tub work their magic. I look down at my state of undress. I hadn't bothered putting clothes back on rather had just pulled on a pair of boxers and settled in the chair to watch a little television. I must have fallen asleep.

"Finn?"

I turn toward the sound of Rissa's voice. That's what woke me up. My mind is still muddled from dreams and the pills. But I'm not so out of it that I don't realize that she shouldn't be here.

"I'm in the back. Just a second," I call out finally before attempting to stand.

Hours of sitting have turned my knees to jelly and as soon as I'm upright, I list to the side, crashing into the dresser. Bottles of cologne shake and rattle on the top and something crashes to the floor. I grab at the wood awkwardly to keep myself upright.

"Damn it!" I want to scream at my own weakness. But this is something I've had to learn to deal with. My body is unpredictable now and it betrays me regularly.

Then I feel strong arms slip underneath me, supporting me. Rissa's arm curls around my waist and she takes my weight against her as she helps me to the bed. She has me sitting before I can protest the help. It doesn't mean I don't resent needing it though.

"Rissa? What are you doing here?" I'm aware that the question comes out grumpy as hell and not at all the appreciative thank you that I should be sending her way.

It doesn't seem to faze her. Once she's convinced that I'm steady, she takes a step back. "I heard you fall."

"I'm okay. I was just sitting for too long. But actually that wasn't what I meant. I meant, why did you come back? Unless my sense of timing is really off and it's tomorrow morning already."

She smiles slightly. "No, I left some of my supplies here. Then I heard the noise. Well, I was worried about you."

I'm not too weak to feel ashamed as her gaze roams over the scars on my chest and my bare leg revealed by my boxers. The thought that she might feel sorry for me is almost too much to bear. I'd rather have her fight me, yell at me, or even walk away before I'd ever have her look at me with pity.

"You remember what I said would happen if you stepped foot in this room?"

Her eyes suddenly turn wary. Her hands are still on my shoulders so she snatches them back. I snag one of her wrists and pull her closer. She stumbles and lands against me.

"You should have listened."

Then I yank her against my chest hard and take her lips in a bruising kiss.

Despite her initial surprise, her lips part immediately for the thrust of my tongue. If I thought that I was going to dominate and take over, I was wrong. Rissa melts against me like whipped cream and she's twice as sweet. She leans against me using my body to support her so she can curl one leg up around my waist. Then she straddles my lap and I can't stop myself from grinding against her. I nip down her neck, breathing in her fresh scent. Just the way she smells brings up so many memories. I take her lips again and our tongues duel before she finally pulls back, her hands in the center of my chest to hold me back.

"Why are you doing this, Finn?"

"There was a time when I believed that we were meant for each other. You told me that you'd always be mine and that together, we'd make our way in the world. Well, those days are long gone but the time has come for you to make good on at least some of that. I want what you promised me. I want you to make this place a home."

She looks horrified by what I'm saying and there's a part of me that knows this is exactly what I deserve.

"So you're doing this to punish me?" she gasps.

"Yes. But I'm doing this just because I want to." Then my hands travel down over her back to land on her full curvy ass. As I squeeze the round globes, she whimpers into my mouth.

The sound seems to wake her up because she pulls away and stares at me. "I wish I knew if this was real or if it's just one more way for you to hurt me." She disentangles herself from my grip and then hustles from the room.

"I wish I knew too, angel."

Chapter Four

Rissa

Several unopened boxes of wet wipes fall from the shelves above me, pelting my arms and neck. With a curse, I bend and pick them all up before stuffing them back in their storage container. For the first time in a year, I have a chance of being able to find what I need in the crowded storage room without a map, a prayer and three wishes from a genie.

"Uh oh. You only organize like this when you're upset."

I pause in the act of stacking the boxes of rubber gloves by size. "I'm not upset. This place is just filthy."

And I need to do something to take my mind off vengeful millionaires and mind-numbing kisses.

"Did Andrew call again? You'd tell me if he did, right?" Tara's voice is hushed. It's after six in the evening and I'd assumed there was no one else in the building. Apparently I was wrong if Tara is still here.

"No, I haven't heard from him since I hung up on him." I mess with the boxes again. Suddenly the need to tell someone outweighs my embarrassment at being in this situation. I turn to Tara. "Do you remember what I told you about my life before I met Andrew?"

Tara perches on the edge of the desk. "Yeah, I remember you said you had a hard time."

I shove the eco-friendly toweling we use farther back on the shelf. "You're being kind. I was poor. Dirt poor. Mom worked really hard but she was on her own and we considered it a step up when we moved to the trailer park."

"And then you met Andrew."

"But before him, there was someone else. Someone I dated in high school."

Tara's eyes gleam. "Wait a minute. You've never told me this before! You had a high school sweetheart?"

"I've never told anyone this before." I pick at the edge of one of the cardboard boxes until it rips down the side. Finally I turn to face Tara.

"His name was Finn. He was from the neighborhood, too so he understood what it was like to be looked down on by the other kids. Not that anyone made fun of him." I laugh aloud thinking about

Finn in high school. "He was the type of guy who could make friends with anyone. He was so … perfect. That was how I always felt around him. Like how could this perfect guy fall for *me*?"

Tara makes a face. "Of course he fell for you. You're awesome."

"I wasn't awesome back then. I was insecure and just … so stupid. I didn't trust in what we had and when he went into the Army, I don't know. It was just so hard. Finn was the type of guy that women love. And he loves them back, you know? And then I met Andy and he seemed so stable and so safe. That was what I wanted more than anything. Just someone that I could trust to be there for me."

Tara watches me as I come sit next to her on the desk. "What happened, sweetie?"

"I left him. Told him that it wasn't going to work out. I broke his heart."

Tara sighs. We sit just like that for a while before I work up the courage to finish. "The new client. The jerk. It's Finn."

"Oh boy."

"Apparently he's some rich big shot now and wants to torture me by making me clean and decorate his million dollar fuckpad."

"Maybe he wants you back? He might sound like he's angry now but he went through a lot of trouble to get you in his life again. Maybe this is his twisted way of reconnecting?"

"He just wants to rub my nose in the fact that he's wealthy now." I can't even keep the self-pity out of my voice.

Tara looks stricken. Then she suddenly jumps to her feet. "You know what? He can stuff his contract. You don't need this. We can always find a few other contracts to replace this one. We were fine before and we'll be fine again."

"We're not fine. We're barely hanging on. If we want to keep our business running and for all our employees to keep pulling paychecks, I'm going to have to take one for the team."

Tara doesn't look convinced. "I wouldn't blame you if you wanted to walk away. Just say the word. You've always supported me when I needed you and I know Daphne would say the exact same thing if she were here."

I think about what she's offering for only a split second before I discard the idea. Although I know that Daph and Tara would essentially bankrupt themselves to keep me away from Finn, I wouldn't be any kind of friend if I let them do it. This is my mess. And I'll be the one to clean it up. Literally and figuratively.

Maybe this is my chance to finally clean the slate of my past and offer heartfelt amends for my mistakes. Only then will I ever be able to move on.

"No, but thank you. I can deal with a vengeful ex for that amount of money. There's nothing he can do that would be worse than what I did to myself."

* * * * *

When I arrive at Finn's place on Monday morning I'm armed with industrial strength rubber gloves and the determination not to let anything he does get to me. I used the weekend to get my head on straight and now that I know what's going on, there's no point in trying to make nice or ask for forgiveness. Finn needs to punish me for the way I hurt him years ago and I can't pretend I don't understand his desire to do so.

All I can do is grin and get through it because I need this contract even more than he needs closure.

I push the door open and the smell hits me first. As I walk past the kitchen it's so strong that I have to cover my nose with my hand.

What the hell crawled in here and died?

I turn around and take in the rest of the apartment with growing dismay. There are clothes strewn all over the place, even on top of the television. There's something hanging from the bookcase that appears to be a sock and the air is rife with the stench of old alcohol bottles even though I don't see any. I guess he threw those away at some point.

Did he have a party over the weekend? Finn used to be the type that I could imagine hosting a drunken rager any day of the week but the man I met last week seemed more sedate than that. Then I remember his last words to me.

So *this is how it's going to be*. He means to punish me and this is how he's going to do it.

Once I walk in the kitchen and look down at the counter, I discover the culprit. Finn must have had a tuna sandwich yesterday and left the remains out overnight.

Ugh. He's clearly committed to his make-Rissa-pay plan because the trashcan is right below the counter where he left the funky sandwich. I think it actually might have taken him more effort to leave it on the counter than if he'd just done the proper thing and thrown it away.

I blow out a sigh and survey the room. With a mess like this, it honestly doesn't even matter where I start so I just pull on rubber gloves and unroll a trash bag. I walk around the room picking up debris. In some cases I'm not even sure if what I'm picking up is in fact trash but I'm not going to worry about it. He's paying me to clean not think. Plus, he's clearly rich enough to replace anything I accidentally throw away.

And this place is going to be spotless when I'm done. If he's hoping to find fault with my work so he can void the contract, then he's not getting that satisfaction. This place is going to be so clean that it would even pass my mother's white glove test.

For the next hour, I work steadily. Most of it was surface damage. I'm pretty sure Finn just took a bag of laundry and tossed its contents as far as he could reach. But underneath it all, the place really isn't dirty since I just cleaned it a few days ago. So after my initial sweep to get all the trash, I herd all the dirty clothes into a pile and wipe down all the surfaces. After that, I tackle the hall bathroom. When I poke my head in the guest bedroom, I'm hesitant, worried that he might have trashed it too. But it looks the same. The bed doesn't look like it's been touched. I dust the night tables and the headboard quickly before poking my head in the office. The only things in the room are a desk and chair. It doesn't take long to wipe them down.

All in all, the place looks pretty good. I'm surveying my handiwork with a satisfied smile when Finn appears.

When he sees me standing in the living room, he nods. "Oh you're done. Good. I need you."

"I'm already finished cleaning."

He smirks. "You didn't read the contract did you?"

I clench my teeth together to keep in the smart remark on the tip of my tongue. What the hell is up with everyone and this damn contract?

"Yes, I read it."

"Then you know I own your time between the hours of eight and twelve."

"But I'm done." I gesture around the sparkling apartment. All of the furniture has been restored to its rightful positions and all the surfaces gleam. I'm not sure what else he thinks I can do in here.

"Not here. We're going out. I need new stuff. And you're going to help me choose it."

My patience finally snaps. After working for the past two hours straight, my back is screaming and my feet hurt. I want to smack that grin right off his face, contract be damned.

"You know what, no. You are paying me to clean. You want to trash your own apartment just to get back at me, real mature by the way, that's fine. You want to make me pick up your skanky girlfriend's underwear and show off how many Magnum condoms you've used in the past few days, that's fine too. But I'm not some dog that you can snap your fingers at and expect me to follow. I may work for you but you don't own me."

His eyes burn as he steps forward. "Oh yes I do. I didn't write that contract to buy a cleaning lady. I did it to buy you. For the next six months between the hours of eight and twelve, you are mine."

I'm so frustrated that his harsh words bring tears to my eyes. I hate that I cry when I'm angry. I want to be strong and yell back at him but this kind of fury makes me feel very small. "I am not yours. I'm not anybody's."

He stalks forward again and I instinctively shrink away. He doesn't seem to notice. He rests his forehead against mine, the harsh rasp of his breath hitting my cheek. When he pulls me closer, I am too stunned to protest.

"You are mine just as much as I am yours. This hold you've had on me has gone on too long. You walked away from me but when you left you took a part of me with you. I haven't been able to sleep without you walking in and out of my dreams. I can't close my eyes without feeling your presence. You're always with me. I can't live like this anymore."

His lips feather over my forehead and the frustration I feel morphs into a different kind of ache altogether. Maybe this is part of his plan, to hold me the way he used to and make me feel all the things that no other man has ever made me feel.

"You want revenge for the way I treated you. I know that. And you won't believe me but I am truly sorry for the way I left things. You deserved so much more than that. So much better than me. It's better if I assign someone else to come here so we don't have to see each other. It's just hurting us both."

He looks down at me. "If you do that I will void the contract and tie you up in court so long you'll go bankrupt just from all the legal fees. Don't push me on this, Rissa. You have no idea how far I'm willing to go."

"Is this really what you want? It's not healthy for you to keep all this anger inside. You have to move on."

"That's just it angel, I can't move on until my heart accepts the true nature of who you are. A girl who could ditch me for a richer guy and not look back. But the only way that'll happen is if I spend time with you. So you are going to go where I need you to go. You are going to talk to me. *And I am going to purge you from my fucking system or I'll destroy us both trying.*"

* * * * *

I tuck my hands under my legs again as we ride along in silence. We're being driven somewhere, Finn wouldn't tell me where, in the back of the most gorgeous car I've ever seen. It takes all my willpower not to reach out and touch all the shiny surfaces. The things he said to me, no growled at me, are swimming around my head. I'm offended by the fact that he feels he has essentially bought me like a horse but even more, I'm entranced by his assertion that he needs to purge me. That he's obsessed with me after all this time.

I shouldn't have felt such a thrill of pleasure when he said that. Finally I can't take the silence anymore. "You have a Bentley?"

He chuckles. He's sitting on the other side of the seat with his cane between us. The car is so spacious it almost feels like I should be yelling so he can hear me.

"I haven't had it long. I found that driving on this leg some days is painful." He looks at me speculatively. "I don't remember you being into cars."

"I wasn't but you were. I paid attention some of the time." Our eyes meet and there's this strangely soft expression on his face, like he's remembering.

"You always noticed everything. You always seemed to know when I was upset about something." He looks away, out the window to the traffic rushing past.

Thinking about the past doesn't help us, it only mires us in all the things we did wrong. I cough and bring us back to the reason why we're here.

"Okay so you need stuff."

"I do. House stuff."

"That doesn't tell me anything. What kind of stuff do you need? Couches, chairs, dining table. What?"

"Honestly I don't know. The place came partially furnished and I haven't cared to do much since then. I've been recuperating."

His hand lands on top of the head of the cane. He toys with it absently as he talks. I'm struck again with the intense desire to know what happened to him. To hear him talk about his life after we parted, as if knowing can somehow erase all the time and distance between us.

"It looks great already just a little empty. There's no artwork on the walls and the dining area is empty. It feels like a model home, not a place where someone actually lives."

"That's what we're going to fix."

The scenery outside has changed to a more rural landscape. We pass through an area with large, stately homes and well-manicured lawns. We're not in Norfolk anymore or at least not any part that I've ever seen. The car finally slows and turns on a narrow lane. A large Victorian style home appears at the end of the drive. It looks like a dollhouse.

"Where are we?"

"In West Haven. There's an artisan furniture store here that my lawyer recommended. One of the things I like to do is buy local. If at all possible, I use local craftsmen and workers for anything I do."

The scary guy who has been driving us opens my door and I scramble out. There are large oak trees bordering the drive and the air is soft and cool as a kiss beneath their shade. I follow Finn up the drive. A soft bell tinkles overhead as we open the front door.

As soon as I step over the threshold, I feel like I've been transported back in time.

"Wow. This looks like the set of some historical film about the antebellum south."

Heavy drapes, currently tied back with rope tiebacks, adorn the windows. The hardwood floor shines beneath faded rugs that look like they cost as much as the Bentley sitting in the driveway.

The proprietor, a friendly older man who introduces himself as Franklin, takes me on a tour of the main showroom, explaining the significance behind some of the pieces. They deal in antique restoration and they also carry originals crafted by local artists. I wander around lost in fantasy. When I look up, Finn is standing in the same spot by the door. He's not looking at the furniture.

His eyes are all for me.

Finally he makes his way over to where I'm standing. "What do you think?"

I answer honestly. "I think this place is fantastic."

"Now that you've had a chance to look around, has anything caught your eye?"

"Just the entire store!"

He laughs at my exaggerated sigh of pleasure. "If you could have anything in this store you wanted, what would you choose?"

I look around the store, all the choices suddenly three times as tempting now. "What's my budget?"

"There is no budget. Whatever you want. Just pick out what you think would look good in my place."

A bright turquoise chaise lounge catches my eye from across the room. I walk in that direction with Finn right on my heels. When we stop, I gesture at it dramatically. "This looks like a showstopper, huh? I'm thinking we might need more than one of these."

His expression is so shocked that I can't stop the giggles rising up. "Maybe we should even get one for your room!"

"Bright colors have never been my thing but I agree, this is really … something." When he sees me laughing, his expression changes and he looks like he's about to laugh too. "But seriously, I want you to choose things that you really like. Pick everything you'd choose if you were decorating your own place." He runs a fingertip over the curved back. Inexplicably, my back arches and moves as his finger moves, like the action is directly connected to my nerve endings.

"But it's not my house. You're the one who has to live there."

"True but if I decorate it'll look like a cross between an army barracks and a frat house. That's what you're here for."

"I'm here so you can torture me. That's the reality, Finn." Suddenly I'm tired of the back and forth, the wondering and the disappointment of not being able to just enjoy this time with him at face value. Every moment I have to be aware that I'm here only as long as he finds his revenge game amusing.

"That's not all of it." Suddenly he looks uncomfortable. "It's not just about revenge. It's about promises unfulfilled. You promised me once that you would help me make a home. I'm holding you to that. Even though nothing else we promised seemed to matter."

"It wasn't like that. Loving you was a risk I wasn't mature enough to handle back then. You're the guy who loves to flirt and always has a compliment for every woman he meets. How was I supposed to compete with that? I grew up seeing what men like that leave behind. Kids and moms who have to work three jobs. That was our life and I wanted something more. I wanted stability. I wanted something real. So I chose the man who I thought could give me that."

"Let's not split hairs. You left me for the guy who could give you the big house and the fancy car and the rock on your finger. You chose the guy who could take care of you."

"I take care of myself! I always have. But everyone needs someone to fall back on. Someone they can trust to be there. That was why I left you. You aren't the guy who sticks around, Finn."

"I would have for you. *I would have stuck for you.*"

"All of this is in the past, Finn. What's the point of arguing about it now? It doesn't matter. Andrew is part of my past. And so are you."

"Your past?"

"We're not together anymore," I admit. "I'm sure you already know that."

Finn stares. "I didn't. I just assumed you were still together. You're living in his house."

"Because he gave it to me. As an incentive not to talk to the press. We can't have anything tarnishing the Carrington name, now can we?"

He opens his mouth to say something else but I hold up a hand to stop him. I'm so tired of talking about Andrew. He's out of my life and I refuse to allow him to take up any more of my time.

"It doesn't matter. We're here to pick out some furniture. So let's do that. You hired me to do a job so let me do it. No more talking about the past. Okay?"

He nods, looking like he's in a daze. But when I turn to walk away, he follows.

Chapter Five

Finn

I've gotten used to the soft sounds Rissa makes when she's working. But this time when I open my eyes it's to the sound of screaming. Not sure whether what I heard was part of a dream or nightmare, I sit up slowly, my senses on alert. I was up all night thinking about Rissa's stunning declaration yesterday that she's not with Andrew anymore. She's single.

She's mine.

It's impossible to stop my mind from leaping to the most ridiculous end of the spectrum, imagining that because she's free it means that I can have her. Then I hear it again. A scream coming from the living room.

I roll to the side and stumble out of bed, hissing in a harsh breath as all of my weight lands on my right leg. I breathe in and out in shallow pants as the pain slices through me. Then I make my way down the hallway, holding on to the wall for leverage.

Another high-pitched shriek cuts through the early morning silence and I power on, my muscles screaming every step of the way. It hurts but I have to get to her. I have to protect her.

I barge into the living room, ready to charge, attack and dismember whoever the hell has hurt her. But the sight that greets my eyes is so unexpected that instead I stop suddenly.

"Tank? What the hell are you doing?"

The question halts my brother in the act of spinning Rissa around on his shoulder. Like two children caught in the act, they both freeze and look over at me. Rissa looks up from her perch on Tank's shoulder, her hair hanging over her face and down Tank's back. The big smile on her face slowly fades.

"What the hell is going on?" I ask again since neither of them seems interested in giving me an answer.

Tank puts her down and once she's steady on her feet, Rissa yanks her shirt down and glares at him. "Your brother hasn't gotten the memo that we're adults now. He thinks he can still lift me up and spin me around to try to make me puke!"

Completely unrepentant, Tank grins back at her. "Old habits die hard."

Rissa tries to maintain her stern expression but finally a smile spreads across her lips. "I thought your brain would have finally caught up with that big body by now but it seems you're still thirteen years old inside."

It kills to see her smiling at him, giving my older brother everything she's been denying to me for the past few days. Every smile she sends my way is forced and tinged with sadness but the first time she sees Tank she lights up like a goddamned Christmas tree?

I grit my teeth resisting the urge to throw them both out. "Some people are still sleeping at seven am."

Tank snorts. "If you're sleeping when a woman this fine is in your place then you're doing it wrong, bro."

Rissa flushes as red as her hair. "Tank, it's not like that. Your brother hired my company to clean this building."

"Oh you have a cleaning business? That's awesome."

"Yeah, I do." Her pride comes through in every word. She rushes over to the couch where she's left her things and reaches into one of her bags. "Here's my card in case you ever need cleaning services or you know anyone who does."

Tank takes the card and slips it into his pants pocket. "I'll definitely do that. I work for Alexander Security and my boss is in the process of building a satellite office down here. I'm sure he'll need a cleaning company then."

"Really? That would be great. I'm really glad I ran into you again!" Rissa is practically dancing where she's standing. And she's looking up at Tank like he's just promised to personally bankroll her entire operation. All he's done is promise to pass on some information.

"Why are you here, Tank?" Not that it's unusual for my brother to visit but it's rarely this early in the morning.

The faintly guilty look on his face tells me that he was hoping to catch me home so he could force me to talk. I've been dodging him for weeks now, only seeing him in passing at Mom's bedside. But I'm not ready to have some kind of heart-to-heart with my brother where he asks a bunch of questions that I'm not ready to answer.

"I just wanted to check on you." He glances over at Rissa and then his smile is back. "But it looks like you're in good hands. So I'll get out of here and back home to my lady. If I'm lucky, she hasn't woken up yet and I can get in a cuddle."

I scowl when Rissa practically melts at his feet. She beams that bright smile up at him again.

"Aww, that is so sweet. What a lucky girl."

"Yeah, yeah. Get out of here. And next time, call first." I'm not sure why I add that last part but Tank seems to take it as some sort of confirmation that Rissa and I are dating again.

He gives me a knowing grin before looking over my shoulder. "It was great seeing you again, Marissa."

"You too –" Her reply cuts off abruptly when I shove Tank out into the hallway and slam the door. "Finn! That was rude."

"What's rude is him coming over here at the crack of damn dawn and waking me up by flirting with my cleaning lady."

She just rolls her eyes and moves across the room to where she left her supplies. As she rummages through bags and pulls out gloves and a spray bottle, I move to the kitchen. It's awkward just to stand here and stare at her, so I pretend that eating breakfast this early in the morning while I'm still in my boxers is totally normal.

I take down a box of cereal and pull a bowl from the cabinets. She only glances my way briefly before she moves over to the living room and starts spraying the surfaces with whatever's in her spray bottle.

Even though I want to punish her, I also have this driving need to talk to her. To see if what I remember was ever real. Because she can't be as open and real as she seems, as the girl I remember. She has to be something else because the girl I fell for wouldn't have done what she did to me.

Finally I remember that I had some paint samples delivered for her to look through. They're on the counter next to yesterday's mail. I grab the envelope and shake out the contents. Rissa looks up when I approach.

"What do you think of these colors?"

"For ..." She gives me a strange look.

I gesture around us. "For this room. It's kind of boring in here now. I thought a coat of paint might liven things up a bit." I hold up one of the chips. It's a soft tan color. It's labeled Afternoon Espresso. Why are paint colors always reminiscent of food?

"What about this tan color?"

She moves closer and her scent washes over me. Rissa was never fond of perfumes, choosing instead to just use scented soaps and shampoos. She smells just the way she did back then, fresh with a soft hint of something fruity. It brings back memories of the cherry-flavored lip-gloss she used to wear and that I used to have smeared all over me.

"If you paint it that color, it'll likely still look very monotone in here. Most of your furniture is dark so I'm thinking you need some color."

I agree so I shift to the bolder tones in the bunch. I pull out one of the more outlandish ones.

"What about this blue?"

"I'm not so sure about that shade. It's a little Disney for my tastes."

Although I can see what she means, I persist, mainly because I enjoy how her chest bounces up and down when she gets worked up like this.

"Maybe I like that whimsical sort of look. I could go for an Aladdin theme in here. Maybe turn it into a harem." I smirk at her resultant sigh.

"Okay, let's do the blue. I'll even stencil a genie on the wall if you want me to, free of charge."

"Generous of you. But I'm actually going to just stick with the tan color. If you can handle sorting out a local painting crew, that would be great."

She snatches the paint chip from my hand. "Why did you bother to ask my opinion if you already knew what you wanted?"

"Isn't that what husbands do?"

The question seems to take her off guard. But now that I've had time to think about it, I know what I need to get over her. For a time

I was so sure that she'd be with me through anything. I deployed knowing that she was safe at home waiting for me and that knowledge carried me through. It made it a little bit easier to leave knowing that she was what I was fighting to protect. Then to come home and find every dream that sustained me was a lie ... Well, I think over time my mind turned that dream into an obsession. I need to prove to myself that it doesn't have any power over me. That being with her, being her husband isn't what I always thought it would be.

I have to know what it's like to have her at my side, just for a little while. Maybe then I can finally purge this obsession.

"Husband?" she squeaks.

"Well, that's sort of what we're doing. Playing house. Just the way we always dreamed. I can finally give you everything I couldn't then. All the things you obviously needed."

Her mouth drops open. "That's not what it was about. It wasn't about things."

"Of course it was. I'm not angry anymore Rissa. I understand now. You were just searching for a better life and you took the sure thing. I wasn't a good bet. But now I am and I want to experience all the things that were denied to me when you left. You were engaged and you two lived together so I'm assuming you'll know better than I will. So I'm asking you, isn't this what husbands do?"

"No. Not in my experience. They usually let you think you have a choice and then..."

"And then ... what? Don't tell me you didn't have old Andy boy wrapped firmly around your little finger?"

She glances at me in alarm but it was suddenly the most important thing in the world that she answer this question. I have to know what kind of lover Andrew Carrington was. Because if the golden boy with his fancy suits and Ivy League education hadn't been enough to keep her happy then what chance would I have had?

"No, definitely not. He never had any problem saying no to me." Rissa suddenly looks like she's on the verge of tears.

"What does that mean?"

She whirls around, her eyes bright with tears. "I was never happy with him, okay? He was an asshole and he had me completely fooled. Is that what you want to hear?"

My stomach clenches. I wait to feel some sense of vindication. This is what I wanted at the start of this after all. I wanted to make her see that she chose wrong and that I was the better bet all along. But seeing tears in her beautiful blue eyes isn't any kind of victory.

And the sense of shame I feel for deliberately hurting her makes me feel lower than that shit you find in the crevices of your shoe.

"Rissa—"

"So we're going with the tan color? I'll coordinate for painters to come in. Unless you already have a company in mind?"

She holds up the paint chip. Her eyes warn me that she's done talking about anything personal. Every time she shares a part of her life with me and then pulls back, it's like losing her all over again. But even though it hurts, I know not to push any more.

"No. I don't have any company in mind. You can choose whoever you like."

For the rest of the morning, she cleans around me and dodges every attempt to coax her back into conversation. When I go to my room to dress, she's gone when I come back.

* * * * *

Later that day, I'm sitting in my usual booth with Luke glaring daggers at me. Then he suddenly narrows his eyes.

"What's wrong with you?"

"Nothing is wrong with me. I'm here just like I am every other damn day, aren't I?"

My tone should have put him off but it seems to amuse him. "You're crabby. You didn't even flirt with the waitress when she dropped off your pie and then there's the absolute proof that something is up."

"Oh yeah, what's that Sherlock?"

He points at my plate. "You still have pie left. In the entire time you've been harassing me, a piece of pie has never survived this long on your plate."

"I'm starting to understand why most people think little brothers are annoying."

Suddenly he sits back. "Don't tell me a girl has you like this?"

His statement hits a little too close to home. "You're just a kid so I wouldn't expect you to understand."

"I'm not a kid. I'm twenty-two." He says this with the kind of pride you can only have when you're that young. Not that I'm so much older at twenty-five but next to Luke, I feel like a bitter, washed up old man.

"Yeah yeah. You'll be on Depends before long."

"This girl must be something to have you looking like that. I mean, if even the pie hasn't cheered you up."

It makes me think. Why is Rissa affecting me this way? The whole purpose of this is to get her out of my system. To show her how wrong she was and make her regret her decision. It was supposed to make me feel better and give me closure. But there's nothing final about how I feel for her.

"What's so special about this girl anyway?" Luke is watching me with genuine curiosity.

It makes me uncomfortable. Like I'm some kind of math problem that he's trying to solve.

"She used to be everything and then she was nothing."

Luke is staring at me with newfound interest. "Damn, man. That's deep. It sounds like she ripped your heart out."

"Don't trust women. That's what they do. They rip your heart out."

"What are you telling my baby?"

I jump when Anita appears at my elbow. Luke just gazes back at me innocently like *this is all on you.*

"Nothing. Just telling him again how lucky he is to grow up eating like this." I give Anita my most charming smile. She just raises an eyebrow.

"Are you taking care of yourself?"

Great, now I have both mother and son watching me like I'm at risk of slitting my wrists any moment. All the hovering is making me claustrophobic. Coupled with all the worry coming my way from Tank, I'm starting to think all this family togetherness has a serious downside.

I smile up at Anita. "Haven't you figured out why I've been coming here all this time? I'm hoping you'll take me home with you."

"Seriously, you're flirting with my mom?" Luke looks disgusted. "All right. I'll meet your brother if it means you'll stop flirting with my mom. And the other ones. Just don't expect some big happy family reunion or whatever. I mean, do they even know about me?"

"Yes, they all know about you."

The bell above the door tinkles and I look up. Over his shoulder I see Tank. Then Emma. A few moments later, Sasha follows behind.

Shit.

"What's wrong?"

Clearly I must have said what I was thinking out loud. So I don't even try to prepare an explanation. He wouldn't believe it and I wouldn't have time to deliver it. Tank sees me and he turns to say something to Emma. We've only got maybe sixty seconds before they descend on us.

"I didn't plan this I swear."

Luke glances over his shoulder. When he turns around, his face has turned to stone. "Coincidence right? Does he just happen to have a pie fetish, too?"

"He knows I've been here bugging you but I didn't think he was going to just show up. This is not his style at all. It's probably Emma's idea. His girlfriend."

"Great. He's staring. Did you tell him I was black?"

Anita looks mortified. The tops of her cheeks turn red beneath her cinnamon complexion. "Luke! I'm sure they don't care about that."

"Is that why you've been holding back? I wish you'd told me. That doesn't matter to any of us. Not in the way you're thinking anyway."

Luke sits back with a smug smile on his face that looks far too mature for his age. "Let me guess. Some of your best friends are black, right?"

"Not my best friend but my most beautiful friend, definitely. Actually it's funny you should say that because here she comes now."

By this time, Sasha has made it to our table. Before I can even open my mouth to greet her she throws herself into my lap. "Finn! I only tagged along because Emma told me you'd be here. Thank you so much for that referral. I got the job!"

It's hard to keep track of what's going on with a lap full of curvy gorgeous woman but I make an attempt to keep us upright. I'm aware the entire time of Luke's stunned silence as he watches us.

"You're welcome, sweetheart. Trust me, I was doing them a favor. They'll be lucky to have you."

Sasha finally releases the stranglehold she has on my neck and slides into the booth next to me. "Still, thank you so much." She finally seems to notice that we're not alone. She blinks at Luke and Anita. "Oh, hello."

"Sasha this is my little brother, Luke."

Luke is still staring at her with his mouth hanging partially open. If his eyes get any bigger, they'll take over his face.

"Uh, hi." He gives her an awkward wave.

Sasha doesn't seem to notice his discomfort. "This is your little brother? Oh is this the brilliant one? It's so nice to meet you!"

Luke glances over at me again. I decide to throw him a lifeline. "Yes, this is the brilliant one. And this beautiful lady is his mother, Anita."

Sasha shakes hands with Anita. "It's so nice to meet you. I know this is kind of a strange situation, what Emma told me about it anyway. But you couldn't wish for better relations than Tank and Finn."

Surprised, I turn to Sasha. In the beginning I got the impression she wasn't too fond of Tank so it's a shock to hear her speak about him so warmly. "Has Tank managed to trick you into thinking that we're good guys or something?"

She rolls her eyes. "Tank is just a big old growly teddy bear. I thought he was so mean when I first met him but he's not like that at all. And when our boss was getting out of line, Tank showed up and took care of the problem for me. Now, I'm not saying he's all bark and no bite. But he saves his bites for the people who deserve it and he stands up for those of us whose teeth aren't sharp enough to defend ourselves."

"I'm glad he was there to stand up for you sweetie. Would you like something to eat while you're here?" Anita has already accepted Sasha as one of her own, I can tell.

"I'll have a piece of this pie just like Finn's having, please. Thank you."

Anita intercepts Tank and Emma before they can approach. She smiles at them warmly, holding out her hand to Tank. I can't hear what they're saying but then they all laugh.

"Your mom is awesome." I look over at Luke. "Seriously, she's handling all of this so well. Does anything faze her?"

Luke shakes his head. "Well, she had to raise me so what do you think?"

Tank reaches the table and stands awkwardly by my side. I speak up, hoping that Luke isn't so pissed that he'll be rude in front of Emma.

"Luke, this is my older brother Tank and the only woman who can make him behave, Emma Shaw."

Tank scowls at my introduction. "Hey. I know this is unexpected. And I'll leave if you want me to."

Luke sighs. "I'm already being harassed by this guy so honestly I expected the rest of you to show up at some point."

That doesn't sound like a welcome to me but apparently he and Tank speak the same language because Tank grins. Sasha hops up so Tank and Emma can sit next to me.

Then she looks down at Luke. "Do you mind?"

He moves over silently, watching her with a look of awe as she slides into the booth next to him.

I have to stifle my laugh with another bite of the pie I've been neglecting. Was I ever this much of an idiot around beautiful women? Then I realize that I'm still that much of an idiot over one woman in particular.

"Are you okay, Finn?" Sasha is watching me with concern. At her question, Tank and Emma look over at me, too.

"He's having girl trouble." Luke smirks.

"I didn't even know you were seeing someone Finn." Emma looks thrilled.

Tank watches me with knowing eyes. I'm sure he's already figured out that the woman screwing with my head is Rissa. Further, I have a feeling he knows my reasons for bringing her back into my life are not at all altruistic.

"There's no woman. There's nothing. Just a nosy little brother with too much time on his hands."

As the conversation turns to general things, my mind wanders back to this morning. Despite the fact that she's available, I can't allow myself to get sucked back into Rissa's spell. It's time to stop playing around. Maybe I don't need revenge. Seeing her in tears this afternoon wasn't satisfying, it was just sad. My desire to hurt her has morphed into an insatiable curiosity about her life. I want to know if she's happy. I need to know all the things I was too blind to notice when I was teenager.

Andrew had the means to give her everything I couldn't but yet she still wasn't happy with him. There's a stupid part of me hoping that it was because she never got over me. The same part of me that once called out for revenge would love to know that thoughts of me haunted her after we parted, providing her with the same torment that kept me in limbo for years.

But there's another part of me, rooted in the heart that loved her that just wants to understand why. I need to understand exactly what he did wrong and what was missing.

And I need to understand what it was about me that drove away the only woman I've ever wanted to stay.

* * * * *

By the time I get back home, my ears are ringing with unwanted love advice. Emma and Sasha took the opportunity to tell me everything that men usually do wrong in relationships. I tried to tell them several times that I wasn't in a relationship and have no intention of being in one but after a while I just let them talk. My brothers both seemed to enjoy watching the girls school me. Or maybe they were just happy the attention wasn't on them.

I take a seat on the couch. That's when I notice the catalogue on the coffee table. Did Rissa leave something behind? The women on the cover are wearing lacy lingerie so I figure she must have had this in her bag and decided to look at it while she was taking a break. I feel like a pervert as I open the cover but I can't deny that I'm curious if she's marked anything. The idea of her wearing one of these sheer pieces of lace is enough to spike my blood pressure anyway but I really want to see the kind of things that she'd choose for herself.

Inside the front cover, there is a sticky note with my name on it.

Finn. Since you asked for help decorating, I decided to pick out a few things for you. I noticed some things in this catalogue that would be perfect for you! Check out the dog-eared pages.

I flip through the pages until I come to the first folded down corner. To my surprise, this page isn't lingerie at all but furniture. This must be a really diverse company to sell lingerie and furniture. I've never seen anything like it.

Halfway down the page, she has circled a black chair with black permanent marker. I tilt the catalogue trying to understand what is so special about this strangely shaped chair. Then I read the description next to Item 2453B and my breath catches. It's described as a Tantric chair. Perfect to support more adventurous positions.

I turn the catalogue over and suddenly the skimpy outfits make sense. Upon closer inspection it's quite obvious that the lingerie is on the risqué side and when I flip back through some of the pages that aren't marked, there is everything from cock rings to giant dildos. I stop on one page and then hastily flip back to the page Rissa marked. I don't have time to think about why any woman would want a giant purple dildo right now.

Rissa has left another sticky note on the page she marked. I bark out a laugh at the hastily scribbled note.

- - Perfect for your overnight guests. Especially the one who keeps losing her panties in your couch cushions!

A few pages over she has dog-eared a section with handcuffs and nipple tassels.

- - These would be perfect wall decor. Very avant-garde, right?

I'm chuckling as I page through the magazine, discovering several other colorful suggestions for my home decorating needs. The damn woman is playing by my rules and beating me at my own game.

I tuck the catalogue under my arm and stand. She's left this for me trying to get the last word. I text Jonah to bring the car around. I know where she lives so I'm thinking maybe I should drop by and let her know I got her message. It'll also be my chance to apologize for making her cry this morning. No woman wants to be reminded of a breakup.

The ride over to her house is quick but pointless. As soon as we pull up and I see the dark house, I remember that she said she works another job in the evenings. I give Jonah the address to her business office. Hopefully I can catch her before she leaves.

Someone is stepping out of the front door of the small building as we pull up. I roll down the window slightly. "Rissa?"

The girl turns and regards the expensive car in silence. I open the door and step out. Her eyes immediately land on my cane before she pulls her gaze away. I smile at her to let her know that I'm not offended.

"You must be Daphne."

I know who she is due to my research not because Rissa ever mentioned her. Getting Rissa to open up about anything has been difficult to say the least. But Daphne doesn't know that. She looks startled that I know her name, and then she relaxes.

"That's me. Who are you?"

I hold out my hand and she takes a tentative step forward to shake it. "Finn Marshall. I'm here to see Rissa."

"Well, I'm sorry to tell you that you've missed her. I guess you're stuck with me instead."

"That's nothing to be sorry about." When I smile at her, she blushes slightly. "Although I was hoping I could catch Rissa before she went home. I wanted to thank her."

Daphne glances behind her at the obviously empty building. "Home? Oh, she's probably on a job still."

"Could I go see her there? I don't mind driving over."

At the look on Daphne's face I can tell she isn't going to give up the location of Rissa's current job easily. I'm happy to see her loyalty and frustrated because she's the only thing standing in my way.

"She's very lucky to have a friend like you looking out for her. But I mean her no harm. She's an old friend from high school and I'm actually one of your clients. As of last week, anyway."

Suddenly her eyes swing to my face. "You're the high-rise?"

I'm not sure why that one piece of information seems so important but if that works for her, I'll go with it. "Yeah that's me. Rissa left some decorating suggestions for me this morning. I wanted to thank her. And I have to admit, I also don't like the idea of her walking alone to her car late at night. I'm sure she'd think that was overprotective but I can't help it."

Daphne bobs her head in agreement. "She *would* think it was overprotective. But then she's stubborn like that."

"When did that happen? She didn't have a problem with me walking her to her classes when we were in high school." The memory makes me laugh a little. Even before we'd been officially dating, I had always walked Rissa everywhere. I wasn't going to take a chance on any of those assholes messing with her when I wasn't around. That had caused problems with the girls I'd dated before her and I still hadn't cared. I'd been a slave to her even then.

Daphne smiles. "Sounds like you're sweet on her."

The description sounds entirely too tame for how I feel about Marissa Blake. I want her, I hate her, I crave her. Thoughts of her have consumed me for years until it seems there's little sanity or rational thought left in me when it comes to her. There's nothing sweet about it. However, there's no expression in the English language that would encompass all that so I just nod. "Yes, I am."

That seems to push her into a decision. With one last glance at my cane she says, "She's at Mercers this time of evening. You know, the big department store."

I don't shop often but I'm well aware of the store. It's one of the only locally owned department stores left in the area.

"Thank you for your help, Daphne. Rissa is really lucky to have a friend like you."

She turns and walks out to the parking lot. I watch as she climbs inside a sporty little green hatchback and then pulls out of the parking lot with reckless speed and seemingly no regard for her personal safety.

I turn back to the car. At this point, I really should just give this up and go home. The gentlemanly thing to do would be to let Rissa go on living her life with no interference from me. There's no way I can go through with the plan I was so committed to just a few days ago. Because seeing her the way she was yesterday at the furniture store, her eyes bright with excitement just brought it all back in a way that was too real. She can't be that girl anymore, that happy laughing girl who used to make me so happy. The only way I've been able to survive at all is believing that girl never existed.

And seeing her show up yesterday had been too much.

But then I look down at the catalogue in my hand and suddenly I'm smiling. Each day used to be so routine and mundane. I did the same things with the same results. There were no surprises. No joy. Now each morning I wake knowing I'll see Rissa again. I haven't taken any pain pills at all today. The pain is still there, it's just that I'm so distracted by everything else going on. There's no way that I can give this up. I'm having way too much fun to leave her alone.

I close the door and sit back. Jonah turns around and looks at me expectantly. "Where to, sir?"

"Mercers. The department store."

Chapter Six

Rissa

I roll my neck, trying to get the kinks out. The floor buffer I've been using for the past hour has made my arms feel almost numb. But the floors look shiny and perfect.

"Good night Miss Blake!"

One of my new hires, a teenage mother named Carrie, waves as she passes by. Getting a janitorial contract for a big local department store like Mercers was quite a feat for my little company and it meant that we'd been able to hire new people for the first time in a year. For our largest clients, Tara, Daphne and I were always present but we usually handpicked team members to work with us. Carrie was energetic and easy to be around. It had been an easy decision to bring her with me on this job.

"Night. Get home to that gorgeous baby."

At the mention of her six-month-old son Caleb, her face lights up. "Yes ma'am. My mom has already put him to sleep but since I'm getting off a little early, it means I can take a nap before his middle of the night feeding."

"Well, good. Give him a kiss for me."

I watch as she skips out the door and to her car parked directly in front of the store. This late there's no cars here except for ours and a dark sedan parked in the middle of the lot. I can't see what type it is from this far away. I wonder if the owner of the store perhaps got a ride home and left his car here?

I put away the buffer and do my final walk through. Everything looks perfect. This is my favorite part of the day, when the work is done and I can look at what I've accomplished with pride. There are a lot of people who look down on janitorial staff but I have pride in what I do. I make things shine.

I punch in the special security code I was assigned to the panel and then lock the front doors behind me with my key. As I'm walking across the parking lot, the door to the sedan opens. A man steps out. My heart speeds up a bit and I start walking faster. Usually Carrie or whomever I'm working with is walking to their vehicles at the same time so I've never felt unsafe here.

"Marissa!"

I halt with my hand on the door handle of my car. As the man walks closer, I notice the slight limp right before his face comes into view.

"Finn? What are you doing here? You scared me!"

The parking lot is uneven and there are a lot of potholes. He's walking slowly, stepping carefully, as he makes his way to where I am. Part of me wants to make it easier for him and just walk his way, close the distance. But the rest of me still remembers his heartless questioning this afternoon. He wants to hurt me by his own admission. So why do I still feel sympathy for him?

"I didn't mean to scare you. I just wanted to let you know that I got your message."

"What message?"

He holds up the catalogue I'd brought back to his place that afternoon. After I'd left, I was so angry. Usually between morning and evening jobs, I go home and rest in between. But I was so stirred up after Finn's interrogation this morning that I drove back to the office to tackle the paperwork on my desk. There were a few invoices that needed to be paid and I was definitely behind on filing. With all that anger energy, I figured if nothing else I'd have a clean desk at the end of the day.

I'd ordered a pair of fur-lined handcuffs from this particular catalogue as a gag gift for a friend's bachelorette party. They still occasionally send me catalogues so when I saw it in my mail, I knew I had to use it. It was too good not to.

"I was just doing what you said you wanted. Being helpful. Wifely and all that."

Finn bursts into laughter and the rumbling sound startles me. It feels like it's been a very long time since I've heard him laugh. Light glints off the head of his cane. This one has a polished silver handle. Considering all that he's been through since he was discharged, I'm guessing it's been a while since he had anything to laugh about.

"A wife that sends me dildo catalogues. Damn, I've hit the jackpot."

Our eyes meet and then we both start laughing.

Finn moves a little closer and then leans against the side of my car next to me. "I want to apologize to you. My behavior earlier today was out of line."

I shrug but his words actually mean a lot. "I was lashing out too. We seem to bring that out in each other."

He leans closer. "It's called passion. We always had more than enough of that."

"We did. Everything between us was so good. Until it wasn't."

Going back and forth isn't getting us anywhere. And as more time passes, the more I wonder why he's insisting on this ridiculous working arrangement. If he wants to rub my face in his wealth, he's already done that. If he wants to show me that I made the wrong choice, that was already accomplished long before he showed up.

"I'm so tired of thinking about what an idiot I was. I've spent the last few years just trying to move on."

"I can't move past this without knowing whether it was even worth it. Why weren't you happy with him, angel?"

I don't talk about this. With anyone. But something in my face must change because he narrows his eyes. "Rissa?"

"So does that mean you liked the chair?"

His brow furrows then he looks down at the catalogue again. "I don't know. I can see how it would come in handy."

Probably with whatever size zero supermodel would fit into the tiny thong I'd rescued from his couch. "I'm sure your many girlfriends will love it."

"There are no girlfriends, Rissa. There haven't been for a long time. Although I'm sure there's a woman somewhere who won't mind looking at this mangled leg, I haven't found her yet."

I will not feel sorry for him. I will not feel sorry for him.

"The women you date sound like bitches. You got hurt protecting the rest of us. So every scar you have just reminds me that I should be grateful just to be here."

His eyes seem to burn in his face as he stares at me. "Maybe I have found the right woman."

I ignore that, knowing he's just trying to rile me up. "So, did that underwear and all those condom wrappers just materialize out of thin air? Or have they just been there a long time?" I make a face at the thought. "You really *did* need cleaning services then, huh?"

Finn doesn't even bother to disguise his laughter. He turns to me, his smile warm. "I was being an asshole. Trying to mess with you. Those underwear probably still had the tags on from when I bought them."

"I think you also accidentally bought them in the children's section. The cashier probably thought you were a perv."

He looks horrified. "They have underwear like that for kids?"

"Disturbingly, yes they do."

He shakes his head. Then stands back. "Anyway, I wanted to come by and apologize. And make sure you got to your car safely. You know I've never liked you walking places alone."

I unlock the car and throw my bags on the seat. "I know. But you can't show up everywhere just to make sure I'm safe."

He looks amused. "Can't I?"

* * * * *

"Anna, I need you to go to the Greenberg's this morning. And Tracy, you'll have to come with me to Mercers tonight, okay?"

I stand in my office staring at my list of employees hoping that I'm just missing something. I woke up to a voicemail from Carrie that her son was sick so I'd come in a little early to see what I could do. One of my best girls is already on vacation this week and looking at this list, there's no way around it. Without Carrie, we are supremely screwed today.

"So, Julie is going to handle the Fulton job by herself then?" Tracy asks.

I look at the schedule again and then rub my face with my free hand. "No, you're right. That's a two-person job. You stay with Julie. I'll handle Mercers alone today."

Tracy and Anna exchange glances but they both nod.

"Carrie's okay, right?" Anna chews on her bottom lip, looking worried. She's not much older than Carrie and I know the two have become friends.

"Caleb is sick again. She left a message this morning that she wasn't coming in. I'm going to call her back this afternoon to check on her."

Anna and Tracy file out the door so Tara can squeeze in to my minuscule office.

"When it rains, huh?" Tara runs her hands over her face. "Someone always gets sick unexpectedly when someone else is already on vacation. It's like an unwritten rule."

"Yeah I know. But we could always handle it before because we didn't have this many clients."

Ever since the night when Finn apologized in the parking lot of Mercer's, we've had an unspoken truce between us. For the past week things have been completely civil. There have been no more condom wrappers or random women's underwear in the couch cushions and he's stopped snapping at me like I'm a dog.

We've just ... talked. A lot.

And I've felt a sense of calm for the first time since he hired us. Like things were on the right track and I finally had everything under control. Things were going great with the business and Finn and I were actually getting along okay. I should have known that peace wasn't going to last long.

Thoughts of Finn bring my mind to the time. I glance at the digital display on the lower right hand side of my computer. "Oh no! I'm late."

Tara moves back as I race around the desk and grab my bag

sitting on the chair in front of the desk.

"I'm sure he'll understand. This was an extraordinary circumstance."

"Maybe but I can't take that chance. It's in the contract. And I don't want to give him any reason to screw around with us. We need this too much."

As I'm jogging down the hall, I hear Tara call out "Don't let him give you a hard time!"

Things have been better with Finn but I still remember vividly how much he enjoyed taunting me about Andrew. He'd had me on the verge of tears that day but then he did the incredibly sweet thing of sitting in his car for an hour just so I didn't have to walk alone to my car at night. It was the kind of thing he would have done when we were teenagers.

Part of me thinks he's just trying to screw with my head by being evil one minute and nice the next. But when we talk, he seems so sincere. He was a sweet boy but he's become an incredible man. As if I need any other reason to regret the stupid decisions of my youth. The more time I spend with him, the more I realize that what I gave up with him would have likely been the best thing in my life.

By the time I get to Finn's building, it's a quarter past eight. I race through the lobby, waving over my shoulder to John, the morning concierge. The elevator seems to take forever and by the time I burst through the front door, my breath is coming fast and hard.

Finn is sitting at the counter in the kitchen eating a bowl of cereal. He looks up when I burst through the door.

"I'm sorry. One of the girls had an emergency. Her baby is sick. I had to rearrange some things."

He doesn't reply just spoons up another bite of cereal.

I wilt a little at that. He doesn't look particularly sympathetic. This is what he does. He appears calm and collected and then he lets loose one of his cutting remarks that can slice you open just as surely as a blade. When he's only messing with me, it's one thing. My ego can take it. But this is about the company's future. All those women who won't have jobs if he decides not to pay us.

"You aren't going to void the contract, are you?"

The spoon lowers and he frowns at me. Now he really looks pissed. "*Christ*, Rissa. I'm not heartless. Your employee, is her baby going to be okay?"

Now that I know he's not angry, I relax a little.

"Yeah, he just has a cold, I think. But it means I'm in for a really long day. Carrie normally helps me at my evening client and there's no one I can pull in to help out. The other girls already have as much as they can handle."

My heart is still racing from running down the hallway so I rest my arms on the counter. Then I rummage through my bag for my phone. Once I find it, I pull up the last employee schedule Tara emailed me. There's got to be someone that I can move around to make things a little easier.

"I'll help you."

Now that gets my attention. I put my phone down on the

counter and peer at Finn skeptically. "You're going to help? Cleaning?"

He looks amused. "Sure. You used to help me with my chores at home, remember? I figure I owe you one."

"This is slightly more complicated than mopping a kitchen floor, Finn. We're going to be covering a large area. Are you sure you want to volunteer? Because if you are, I'm not going to say no. I'm that desperate." I walk to the couch and set my bags down on the floor.

"If it'll help you out, then yes, I'm serious." His eyes fix on mine and I shiver beneath his gaze.

"Yeah, it'll help me out a lot."

"Then it's done. Just let me know what I need to do."

My phone rings. "Can you check who that is? It might be Tara."

He picks it up and his smile vanishes. When he hands it to me, I see the name Andrew. I quickly hit the button to silence the call.

When I look up, Finn is watching me.

This is definitely not something I want to talk about, no matter how much better things have gotten between us lately. I clear my throat. "I'll be back to pick you up around nine then. Usually it takes a few hours to clean the whole store and then I'm out of there by midnight."

He stands. "First, I'll pick you up. My driver will take us over and pick us up at the end of the night. You're already exhausted and I don't want you driving when you're this tired. Second, I want you to relax with me this morning. This place is still perfect from yesterday's cleaning. So sit down and take a load off. We'll watch something on television."

What he's offering is so tempting but a shade too close to charity. He started out wanting to rub my nose in his wealth and now that we've cleared the air he's probably feeling guilty. But I don't take a paycheck for nothing.

"I'm fine, Finn. Really. I don't need to be chauffeured around and I'm not that tired."

"You are. And you already know that I'm a complete ass when I don't get my way. So sit."

He's not going to give up on this, I can tell. So I drop down on the couch and then glare at him. "You're the boss."

He grumbles under his breath. "If that was true, we wouldn't be wasting time watching TV."

* * * * *

Finn turns on the television and we settle on the couch. I grab one of the pillows and squeeze it to my middle trying to pretend that relaxing in a place that looks like a layout for Architectural Digest is no big deal. I'm also determined to ignore what he just muttered under his breath. Things have been different lately but that doesn't mean I trust him yet.

"We can watch whatever you want."

I shrug. "I don't watch much TV. I'm never home when most shows are on anyway."

He tunes it to one of the morning shows. The anchors are talking about the latest bestselling book, something racy with a cover that makes me blush just to look at it.

Finn points at the TV. "Emma has that book. Tank teased her about it until she finally told him that reading hot books is to his benefit. That shut him up pretty quickly."

"I don't get why people think they have the right to shame women for their entertainment choices. And nobody asks men to defend why they're watching the last Mission Impossible or Jason Bourne flick. No one says they must be boring or unfulfilled in their real lives because they like those shows."

"Who says that?"

"Usually jerks on TV. Anyway, all those action movies are way more unrealistic in my opinion and they glorify violence. If you have to portray something unrealistic, I don't see how showing people falling in love is hurting anything."

He glances over at me. "Falling in love is unrealistic?"

The soft tone of his voice lulls me. I know what he's thinking. How can it be unrealistic when we had that? We had in reality what most people only experience in the pages of a book or through soft focus scenes in a movie. But I can't think about that right now so I take the coward's way out and make a joke of it.

"Isn't it? I'm glad it works out for some people but I think for most of us, it's still nothing but a fantasy."

"I hear billionaires in those love books are all the rage. According to Emma's ereader anyway."

I look over at him in shock. "You were snooping?"

He has the decency to at least look embarrassed. "It was right next to me on the table! I don't have one so I just wanted to see how they work. Anyway, I thought it was funny especially since most billionaires are my father's age."

"Well, I think most women who have that particular fantasy are imagining someone more like you." I don't tell him that I know that from experience, since he's been my favorite late night fantasy for years.

"Except like most wealthy men in my age group, I'm not a billionaire. More like a billionaire-in-waiting. I'm set to inherit billions and so are my brothers. There are very few young men who are independently wealthy. Most inherit it."

"That's not nearly as sexy. Let us keep our fantasies, please."

His lashes lower and his gaze turns heated. "Is that what you fantasize about, Ris?"

Suddenly I can barely breathe. How am I supposed to talk about fantasies with Finn sitting next to me looking like a wet dream? I close my eyes but that just makes it worse. I can hear every sound when he moves closer, the soft shuffling when he stands, the whisper of his jeans against the fabric of the couch as he sits down again. When I open my eyes, he's right next to me.

"Finn?" I don't mean it to but it comes out as a question. A plea. This is when I'm supposed to be strong and push him away. He's already admitted that he just wants to get me out of his system. I shouldn't want him at all when I know his ultimate end goal is to use me and then forget about me.

But then his hand slides under my neck and his mouth is on

mine. I'm glad he didn't take it slow and get my permission because I don't want to think right now. I just want to feel and to remember. And kissing him is just like I remember.

A whimper escapes before I can stop it as his lips travel back and forth over mine. Just soft brushes that awaken every nerve ending. Kissing him was always like this, a sensual experience that made me feel like every inch of my skin was alive. I arch up to him, reaching, trying to get him to deepen the kiss but as always he's in firm control. Then he tugs me closer and tilts his head. The angle changes everything.

My lips part willingly under his and his tongue invades my mouth. His taste, *god his taste*, is perfect. My fingers clench against his chest as I resist the urge to grab him and start exploring. Being with him so young had some advantages. I'd had inhibitions but with Finn, I'd never felt insecure. I hadn't worried about whether my ass was too big or if my thighs didn't touch. With the kind of adulation that only a teenage boy can have for a naked woman, he'd made me feel like a goddess. I can remember hours of touching, kissing and cuddling where we'd done nothing but bring each other pleasure.

But we'd been different people then. We were in love. Making love with Finn had always been about showing each other how we felt. This kiss is a tangled web of lust, deceit and anger.

Because Finn doesn't love me anymore.

"Finn, wait. We can't." I push back slightly but can't seem to stop my hands from roaming all over his chest.

He steals one last kiss, his hands tightening slightly on the back of my neck. It doesn't make me feel threatened at all, rather I get a visceral sense of just how much he wants me. He has unresolved feelings of anger toward me for what I did but he wants me still.

"I'm sorry. That really wasn't why I asked you to stay." He moves back slightly. His lips are swollen and I like seeing the evidence of what we just did. I lick my own lips instinctively, getting one last taste of him.

He growls and then whips around to face the TV. It takes a few minutes but eventually my own breathing settles back to normal and we watch the rest of the morning talk show in silence. After it's over, Finn stands.

"I'm going to take a shower. A cold one."

At his words my eyes are instantly drawn to the bulge at the front of his jeans. I don't dare look up at him right now because I have no willpower where he's concerned. I'll just end up joining him and helping him take care of the problem I created.

He hands me the remote. "You can watch something else or close your eyes and catch a nap if you want. But I'd better not find you cleaning when I come back out here."

"Bossy." I whisper the words but if his quick grin is any indication, he hears me anyway. Once he disappears down the hallway, I put my feet up on the couch and close my eyes, instantly reliving our heated kiss. Stopping him was really hard but I know it was the right thing to do.

That day when I ran into his room, he'd warned me then that he meant to have me again. But I'd known then just as surely as I know

now, that his desire wasn't about love, it was about proving a point. It was about revenge. Now that we've cleared the air, I don't think Finn is still trying to hurt me but if I'm not careful that's exactly what will happen.

Making love with Finn is one of the few unspoiled memories I have in my life. I don't want anything to take that away from me.

Chapter Seven

Finn

It's nearly midnight and I am exhausted. I also have newfound respect for Rissa. It's not that I ever thought cleaning was easy. It's more that I had no idea it was this fucking *hard*.

"You can take a break if you need to." Rissa glances over at me. I'm in the middle of tying up another monster-sized trash bag.

Mercers is a pretty big store and we've been over every inch of it in detail. According to Rissa, the employees of the store do general tidying, clean their employee bathrooms and handle vacuuming their individual sections of the store. However, the owners found it more efficient to hire out for the rest of their janitorial needs. So Rissa has assigned me to help her with emptying all the trash bins so she can run the big machine that buffs the floors.

"I'm okay." It rankles slightly to think that she's worried about me. Like I'm some weakling that can't handle a little physical work.

My leg may be compromised but the rest of me is still in pretty decent shape. I heft the bag slightly so I can drag it to the back section of the store. The other one I've filled is sitting there. I'll have to take them to the dumpster out back before we leave.

When I come back, Rissa is just finishing the last section in the main entryway.

"I don't know how you do this every day." I have to yell slightly so she can hear me over the sound of the machine.

Rissa shrugs and then turns the buffer off. "Lots of people have it worse. We all just do what we have to."

I walk over and tip up her chin. "That was a compliment in case that didn't come through. You are amazing."

Her cheeks flush. "I'm used to working hard. I remember that you were the same way."

"I was. Maybe that's part of my problem now. I don't have that same sense of purpose. The accident took that away from me just as much as it took pieces of my leg."

She looks up at me sharply. It's the first time I've talked about my injury to her at all. It's not something that I'm comfortable with myself yet. But I don't want her to think that I'm some lazy playboy just because I have money now.

I brush a finger over the skin of her cheek. Her skin was always perfect. Just like everything else about her. It's part of the reason I've never been able to get her off my mind. Ever since that scorching kiss this afternoon, I haven't been able to think about anything else but touching her again. Kissing her wasn't my intention but she'd been so close and looking at me the same way she is now. Like she's remembering how good it used to be. Damn if that doesn't make me want to show her how much better it would be now.

"I was sorry to hear about you getting hurt. My mom still keeps in touch with some of the people from the old neighborhood. I didn't know exactly what happened, just that you'd been hurt. I wanted to visit you but I didn't think you'd want to see me."

She has no idea. After the accident, I'd been filled with rage. At myself, at fate, at the face that wasn't there. She was the first person I asked for when I woke up in the hospital. My mom told me that later. I was delirious from pain and my first instinct was to call out for Rissa. It wasn't until later that I remembered that she wasn't mine anymore.

"I probably wouldn't have been able to handle it just then. I was a mess."

"You were injured. You were allowed to be a mess." She smiles up at me and then all at once seems to realize how close we're standing. She takes a step back and then looks around. "I guess that's it then. We're done for now."

"That's it?" I try not to sound too excited but I'm definitely ready to get home and sit down. My back hurts and my leg is going to be aching tomorrow for sure. I've pushed too hard and the muscles are already knotted in protest.

"Yeah, let's get out of here. I'm sure this isn't what you were expecting when you volunteered to help but I want you to know how much I appreciate it. Things should be back to normal tomorrow."

"I didn't mind at all." To my surprise, it's the absolute truth. I wouldn't characterize the past few hours as fun but it was good to be around Rissa for so long. It felt like the old days when we'd spend hours after school in each other's company. Usually she'd be doing homework while I was practicing for baseball. Then I'd walk her home and spend a little time flirting with her mom, Gloria, to make her laugh. Those had been good times. Simple times.

It was a relief to be able to remember them without bitterness again.

"Come on, let's go."

"Wait, I have to take the trash out." I walk to the back of the store and heft the two large bags out into the alleyway. The dumpster sits right outside the back door but it still gives me a bad feeling. If I hadn't volunteered to help out, Rissa would have been out here alone at this time of night.

Hell, no. She might not be mine anymore but I can't have her alone in alleys in the middle of the night when any kind of criminal could find her. A few ideas run through my head but none that Rissa will go along with. I could hire her to work for me exclusively and then I'd always know she was safe. There's no way she'd go for that so I think briefly about hiring a companion to work with her. She's proud and won't accept anything she sees as charity but if I help her hire more staff, then there won't be a need for her to work alone ever. There will always at least be someone with her to make sure she's safe.

If the maid I hire just happens to have a background as a bodyguard and assassin, well, Rissa doesn't need to know that part does she?

When I get up front Rissa has put away the buffer and waits by the front door. She locks up behind us as we leave. When we step out into the soft, humid air she raises her face to the sky. "It's a nice night. I used to hate the late shift until I realized that it's so nice to be out when everyone else is sleeping. The stars are mine alone."

I look up too, trying to see through her eyes. This is what she's always done for me. She brings me to a new awareness. Shows me the things that I can't see.

Makes me happy.

"Go on a date with me."

Rissa's head snaps around from where she's looking at the stars. She blinks at me a few times and then huffs out a breath. "What did you just say?"

Feeling slightly foolish for the way I just blurted it out, I scowl. "You heard me. Go out with me. On a date."

She looks like she's not sure whether to laugh or not. "Are you asking me or telling me? Geez, you've gotten a lot bossier over the years."

I move closer. "I used to tell you to do a lot of things. And you liked it."

Her indrawn breath is sexy as hell. I can tell she's remembering too, the erotic commands that had brought us both so much pleasure. She'd always been slightly bashful but so eager to touch, to learn. We'd never had much time together without one of our parents coming home but I'd made damn good use of the time we'd had.

"Do you remember all those study sessions?" I'd climbed under her skirt while she was studying many times, using my teeth to pull her little panties to the side.

She bites her lip. "Yeah. Not that I got much studying done. Or that time when you were supposed to be helping me wash the dishes." Her eyes heat. "It took forever to clean up all that water."

I chuckle, remembering how I'd fucked her from behind as she clung to the counter for support. I close my eyes, the memory of her hot little moans as vivid as the day it had happened. Rissa had always been so tight, like she was made just for me. She'd clamped around me so hard that I'd sworn I was seeing stars and when she'd finally come, she'd splashed her hands down into the sink throwing water everywhere.

"All that passion, all that heat doesn't just disappear. I've missed you, Rissa."

"I've missed you too. But I'm not sure that it makes sense to try again. A lot of time has passed. And I work for you now."

"Fuck it, you're fired."

She bursts into laughter and then rests her fists on my chest. "I'll think about it, okay?"

It's not the enthusiastic agreement I was hoping for but it's a chance.

"Good. I'll drive you home."

* * * * *

When we pull up in front of Rissa's place, there is a light on in the window. A dark shadow passes by and then the curtains move.

"Do you have a roommate?"

Rissa shakes her head. "No, I live alone."

"We should call the cops." I pick up my phone but just as I do the front door opens. It's dark but I recognize the silhouette anyway.

"What the hell is Andrew doing in your house? I thought you said he gave it to you?"

"He did. He's not supposed to be here." Rissa shoves the door open angrily and hops out before I can stop her.

Fuck. I grab my cane and follow her out. There's no way in hell I'm leaving her alone with him. She's mine now and it's time Carrington accepts it.

They're so busy arguing that they don't even notice when I walk up.

"Rissa, come on. You can just stay with me tonight."

Andrew looks over at me and when recognition dawns, his face twists into a sneer. "Marshall. I knew it."

Rissa is so angry that she's shaking. "It's none of your business, Andy. You aren't supposed to be here. That was our deal."

Andrew grits his teeth and looks over at me again. "It didn't take

99

you long to replace me, did it? You fucking slut. *I knew there was someone else.*"

The rage in his voice triggers something in me. The way he's looking at her and talking to her makes me want to punch him in the throat. Especially since Rissa doesn't look at all surprised by the way he's acting. I don't care if he's pissed that I'm here or not. He'd better not ever talk to her like that in front of me.

"Yeah, there's someone else. You didn't deserve her anyway and we both know it. Now back away from her." My hand tightens on the head of my cane and his eyes are drawn to it.

"What happened to you?" I can tell he's trying to estimate just how much of a threat I am with a bad leg.

I lift the cane and swing it around once. He has to take a step back to avoid getting nailed in the face. "War happened to me."

Our eyes meet and something in my face must let him know that a bad leg isn't going to save him from the beat down the rest of me would give him.

When his eyes come back to mine, I smile. He glances over at Rissa. She's moved behind me.

I hold out my hand to her. "Go back and sit in the car with Jonah, angel. I'll be there in a minute."

As she walks back down the driveway, Jonah steps out and opens the door for her. Andrew watches with rage filled eyes and then he looks back at me. Then his eyes dart back over to the Bentley at the curb.

Yeah, I'm here and I've got money too.

"Rissa told me that you'd given her the house as an incentive not to talk about you to the press. But hear me now, I have no such incentive. And if I see you near her again, talking will be the least of what I'll do to you."

"You're trash. You've always been trash and I don't know what you've gotten into lately," he gestures at the car, "but you'll still be trash when that finally runs out. Rissa knows that and I do too."

I chuckle. "What I'm into? It's called having a wealthy father with a guilt complex. I guess you'd know all about that. And it'll be hard for me to run out of billions but I'll certainly give it a try. Maybe I'll start by buying the biggest engagement ring out there and putting it on Rissa's finger. Either way, *stay away from her.*"

I turn and walk down the drive. Jonah holds the door open so I can climb in next to Rissa. When we pull off, Andrew is still standing out front staring at us.

Rissa turns to me. "Why did you tell him that? That there was someone else. Now he'll think that we're … It'll only make things worse. He'll never leave now."

"It doesn't matter if he does because I wouldn't let you go back there anyway. The man is obsessed with you. Not that I can blame him since I am, too. We have a lot more in common than I would have ever thought."

She lets out a sigh. It sounds so defeated that it hits me right in the middle of the chest. "Don't say that. You are *nothing* like Andrew."

"It's true. Not that I want to claim anything in common with that bastard but I understand exactly what's going on here. I know what it's like to be consumed by thoughts of you and because I do, I can't let you go back to that house. There's a reason he told you to stay there and it's not just to keep you quiet. It's to keep you under his control."

"So now I'm going to stay at your house and be under *your* control?" Her eyes flash in the dim lights of the streetlamps as we travel over the quiet streets.

"Haven't you learned by now that if there's anyone in control between the two of us, it isn't me? You have the reins here, Rissa. You always have."

She trembles as she absorbs my words. I pull her closer and she tucks into my chest burying her face into my shirt. I run a hand up and down her back, until her shivers stop. After a few minutes, she lets out a soft sigh and I look down to see that she's asleep.

"I told him all that angel, because it's true. You are mine now." I look out the window, allowing the words to resonate in my soul as I speak them out loud. "And I'll never let you go."

* * * * *

The pain starts before I even open my eyes. It's all over me, slicing through my bones and brings me from dreams to reality in an instant. It's raining outside. I don't even need to get up and check. This bum leg of mine is better than any meteorologist at predicting the weather.

Placing one hand on the mattress beside me, I push over onto my side and breathe shallowly through my mouth. I can tell already that this is going to be a rough day. When it starts this early, it's always a rough day. I glance at the clock. It's three in the morning. I didn't even sleep for two hours this time.

After our midnight tussle with Andrew, I brought Rissa straight upstairs and got her settled. I'd made a joke that at least the guest room was clean now.

Rissa had just laughed. "Well, at least I know that for sure."

She was so tired that she didn't even chide me when I helped her out of her clothes so she could sleep more comfortably. She'd just sat there as malleable as a child as I drew her T-shirt over her head and helped her out of her jeans. She wasn't trying to entice me and her lingerie was just plain white cotton. Nothing seductive. But the sight of her rounded curves in the plain cotton was the sexiest thing I've ever seen.

If she hadn't been tired, I'm sure she'd have noticed my erection pressing against the front of my slacks but she just curled up on the pillow. Then she'd placed her hands under her cheek and gone right to sleep. So trusting. Especially after the restrained violence of the scene with Andrew, it was an honor that she trusted me that much.

I walk slowly toward the bathroom. By the time I get there, I'm already a little shaky and slightly nauseated. My stomach rolls as I toss back four pills with a cup of water. If Rissa weren't here, I'd take a few more and spend the day in a blissful fog but the idea of her seeing me like that ... No, that's not something I ever want her to see. For some reason she still looks at me like I'm some kind of hero and I'm not ready to see that change.

That'll change soon enough when she realizes that you aren't really a good guy. That you weren't seeking her out just to punish her. You wanted to ruin her the way she ruined you.

Even my own conscience isn't on my side this morning since the plan that seemed completely logical a month ago seems pretty twisted right now. I stay just like that, breathing in until I feel a warm wave pass through me. The pills are working.

"Finn?"

The voice comes from my room. I walk out of the bathroom to see Rissa standing in the doorway. She's pulled her T-shirt back on but it's not really meant to be worn alone so a shocking amount of leg is exposed. Her arms are around her middle and she looks so lost standing there.

"You can't sleep?"

She shakes her head. "What about you?"

I point down to my leg. "Just the usual. My leg was bothering me so I had to take some medicine."

She takes a step forward and then halts, like she's just realized that she's in my room. Her eyes meet mine and I know she's remembering what happened the last time she came in here. But that seems like a lifetime ago and I don't want her to have even a moment of hesitation around me. She should never worry or fear when she's in my presence. I want her to always know that. I love her too much to ever cause her to look the way she did tonight.

It should scare the shit out of me, this knowledge that I love her still. But I think I've always known it was true. I just couldn't deal with it before.

"I won't do anything to you, angel. You can come in."

She steps closer and the light from the open window illuminates things just enough that I can see the raw desire on her face. "What if I want you to? Would you do something then?"

"Don't tease me. I don't have much self-control when it comes to you and the little bit I have has been used up trying to keep my hands off you these past few days."

"Stop trying," she whispers. Then her hands are in my hair and her mouth is on mine.

My mind goes blank and all I can do is feel. The pain in my leg fades from my awareness as I'm suddenly completely occupied with the soft, warm curves pressing against my chest.

"Hold on to me."

She wraps her arms around my neck obediently and I march her backward toward the bed. The entire time her mouth is on my neck, my ear and then she's tugging at my T-shirt. Urgency pushes us on, as if we have to do it all, touch it all before our time runs out.

We fall on the bed and I roll so she's on top. It takes the pressure off my leg so I can focus on the most important thing which is pleasuring her. I push her T-shirt up but she surprises me when she reaches down and drags it over her head. She must have taken her bra off sometime during the night because she's completely nude underneath.

Holy hell, I had no idea she didn't have panties on under the short shirt either. My dick jumps to attention beneath her. She looks down in surprise. "I guess you liked that, huh?"

"I like you. Everything about you."

"But I'm willing to bet you're pretty partial to these." She cups her full breasts and lifts them to me like an offering. My mouth instantly goes dry. She's always known that I lose all reason when it comes to her breasts. Just a peek at her cleavage was enough to give me an instant hard-on as a teenager. The man doesn't have any chance at resisting them either because Rissa has filled out even more since then. Her curves overflow her small hands and when she leans over me, her breasts dangle like ripe fruit.

"You're drooling, Finn."

"Come here." I plant both of my hands on her ass and drag her up my chest. She squeals but grabs on to the headboard as I position her over my face. Then she sighs when I lick the soft lips of her sex, fluttering my tongue over her little clit. Her soft moans spur me on until I have my tongue buried inside her and she's riding my face.

"Finn!"

I can tell by her soft cries and the way she's gyrating over my lips that she's close. But it's not enough for her to be close, she needs to be frantic. She needs to be lost in what I make her feel. This was the one thing that was always right between us. The connection I feel to her when I make love to her is so potent, it's always seemed fated.

I clasp her bottom firmly with one hand and then use the other to thumb her nipple. Her breasts are so sensitive, they always have been. She tenses and then cries out, her pussy tightening around my tongue. Nothing has ever made me feel more like a man than the privilege of being the one who puts this look on her face.

She rolls to the side, taking big gasping breaths. When she opens her eyes finally, her lashes are wet from her tears.

"I love doing that. I love seeing you come apart."

Her eyes lower to where my erection tents my boxers. Suddenly she looks up at me with a naughty look in her eye. Then she crawls down the bed until she's hovering right over it. She's so close I can feel the warm heat of her breath on the fabric. My hands clench into fists to keep from thrusting up toward her mouth.

"I want to do that to you. I want to taste you."

She hadn't been too fond of this when we were younger. A part of me wonders if she learned to like it with Andrew but I immediately shut that part of my brain down. We both have pasts. It's just the way it is. But I won't let anything intrude on our private time together.

"Lift up." She raises an eyebrow until I lift my hips, allowing her to pull the boxers down. Then she settles herself between my legs, her big blue eyes locked on the erection stretching up my stomach. She leans forward and licks the underside and my hips lift again, the pleasure so intense that I can't help thrusting into it.

She holds me gently, using her tongue to circle the head. Then she takes it all the way into her mouth, her cheeks hollowing the deeper I go. I'm not sure if there's any sight in the world that can bring a man to his knees faster than this one.

"Do you know how beautiful you look?"

She looks up at me, teasingly, her lips stretched tight around my cock. Her tongue swirls and I clench my teeth. There's no way I can withstand too much more of her hot, sinful mouth before I lose it. And I really want this first time I come, for it to be inside her.

"Come here."

She gives one last final lick to the tip which sends another bolt of sensation up my spine. Then she crawls on top of me. I reach into the nightstand next to the bed and hand her the condom. This next step has to be her choice. I need to know that she really wants this.

She rips the package open and rolls it on slowly. Then she positions herself over me, her strong thighs flexing. I grasp the backs of her legs, until she pushes down and takes me deep in one long stroke. My belly clenches and I worry that I won't be able to hold out long enough to make her come again.

It's vitally important that I see that look on her face again. That's all I want in the world is for Rissa to be happy. Happy with me.

I rub my hands up the temptingly soft skin of her back and then grab on to the long curls flowing down her back. Her eyes pop open and she lets out another one of those little cries.

"You are so sexy. You never even knew what you did to me, did you? You never knew that you were my whole world."

Her eyes find mine and she shivers. "I didn't know. All I knew was that I wanted to be your everything. And I was never sure that I was enough."

The uncertainty in the words make me desperate to make her

hear me, to know it now. I sit up and move us back so I'm propped against the headboard. The motion forces her down harder on my cock and her eyes drift shut as she takes it, her nails curling into the skin of my shoulder. The pain just enhances the pleasure. Pleasure and pain. We love each other and we hurt each other. It's the only way we know how to exist, Rissa and I.

"I was too stupid to show you then but there will never be a day that you don't know it now. I love you. I always have."

She's crying now and the sight of her tears just flays me. I couldn't be more vulnerable right now if she split me open and just yanked my heart right out of my chest. But the time for hedging bets is long past. If she leaves this earth knowing nothing else, she'll go with the knowledge that she's the reason why I breathe.

"Say it. Now. Finn loves me."

Her mouth falls open and she pants when I grip her hips and prevent her from moving. "Finn!" Her erotic cry is filled with desperation and a little bit of disbelief.

"Say it."

"You love me," she mumbles, barely getting the words out before her hips move against mine restlessly.

Her eyes flare as I pull her forward. As she rocks forward, I lift my hips and thrust deep. She throws her head back and screams my name, her internal muscles squeezing and pulsating as her orgasm rockets through her.

I want to hold out, make it last but the intense contractions as she falls apart around me are too much. As I fall over the cliff right after her, I look her in the eyes.

"And you may not be ready for this but I know you love me, too."

Chapter Eight

Rissa

I'm in Finn's bed.

That's the first thing I think when I wake in the morning. The next thing is that I'm warm. Finn has pulled me close and tangled our legs together while we slept.

Too much movement will wake him so I carefully roll to the side and pull my hair from beneath his arm. In sleep, Finn looks so peaceful. There's no trace of turmoil over the life-changing things he said to me last night. He hadn't asked me to talk about it or expected me to say it back. I'm grateful for that because I'm honestly not sure what I'm feeling.

I grab a robe from the closet and then walk down the hallway, trying to be quiet. I'm used to getting up early for cleaning jobs but it's weird to be standing in the middle of Finn's living room in the early morning hours.

What am I doing?

I feel completely lost and alone standing there in my T-shirt and one of Finn's robes.

There's a soft noise behind me and I turn. Finn is standing in the middle of the hallway in his boxers.

"Finn? I hope I didn't wake you."

"You didn't but I woke up and you weren't there." He walks across the room. At times like these when he's tired or caught off guard, his limp is even more pronounced. I look up to find that he's watching me. Watching me watch him. I quickly avert my eyes.

"You can ask."

"What?" I look out the window again, ashamed that he caught me staring.

"It's okay, Rissa. It's you ... so it's okay. You can ask what happened."

"That wasn't ... Okay what happened?" It feels wrong and invasive that I want to know so badly. He's been through hell and I'm sure he doesn't want to relive it just to satisfy my insecure desire to know everything about him.

"It was an IED blast. Our truck was almost shredded and so was my leg. I'm lucky I still have it, actually."

"I'm sorry, Finn."

He pulls me into his arms and rests his head in the crook of my shoulder. "I barely remember it. Some people say that's a blessing. But I'm not sure I agree. Without the memory, it's like I just went to sleep one day and then woke up with pieces of my leg missing the next. It doesn't make sense to me."

I turn into his embrace, nuzzling against his neck. "I understand. Your mind can't process something it has no memory of."

"I remember the day I lost you with more clarity. Watching you walk away. Andrew was waiting for you at the end of the street."

He says each sentence as if by rote, like he's reading a list from a piece of paper. Horrified, I raise my head to look into his eyes. I never knew that he saw all that. My heart clenches at the blank look on his face but I don't let myself look away. I deserve to see what I did to him.

"Walking away from you was the worst mistake of my life. And I know I said it before but I want you to hear it again. I'm so sorry that I hurt you. But maybe it'll make you feel better to know that I hurt myself, too."

Warmth returns to his eyes. "I thought that was what I wanted. I was wrong. Seeing you in pain just hurts more. All I've ever wanted for you was to see you happy. And now that I have a chance to make that happen, I won't let you get away so easily this time."

We stay like that for a long time where he's just doing this comforting stroke over my hair and my nose remains buried in his neck. The events of the past day are catching up with me. Andrew always has a way of appearing in my life when I least expect it and I know that Finn is right. He's using the house to keep tabs on me. I wouldn't be surprised if he's getting reports on what I'm doing from the neighbors. They've known him a lot longer than me and I'm clearly the outsider in the neighborhood. Moving out is a necessary step towards breaking the chains of the past.

"You're right," I whisper.

Finn moves back slightly so he can hear me. "Right about what?"

"Moving out. I'm going to get my own place."

He looks around and I shake my head before he can even say it. "I'm not moving in here so don't even say it."

The smirk on his face is my first clue before he says something outlandish. "Since I fired you earlier, maybe you'd be interested in applying for the newest position available here at Casa Finn. I'm looking for a live-in housekeeper. Know anyone?"

Joy bubbles up and I have to squeeze him tighter to contain it. "I haven't even agreed to go on a date yet and you're asking me to move in? Finn, this is crazy."

He pulls me up on my tiptoes for a soft kiss, his eyes going deep and dark in that way I love. "You *will* be going on a date with me and you'll *definitely* be moving in here eventually. So you might as well just go ahead and do it now."

"Bossy."

Suddenly he's serious. "I know I'm a lot to take on Ris but there's never going to be anyone else for me."

And how the hell am I supposed to resist that?

"Damn it, Finn. How do you always do that? You can make the craziest thing seem like it's logical." He makes me want to do crazy things with him. Because everything I do with him seems so natural.

"Because you know in your heart it isn't crazy at all. It's just the way things should have always been."

* * * * *

We talk all morning, taking a break only to soak in Finn's oversized jetted tub. Then he decides to try an experiment to see how many times he can get me off using the jet streams and his fingers. It turns out having sex in a Jacuzzi is a thing for a reason.

By the time we get out, we're both exhausted, dehydrated and wrinkled like raisins. Finn takes his time drying my skin with a big fluffy towel and then wraps me in another one of his robes. I think he just likes seeing his clothes on me. I like it, too.

After that, he leads me to the kitchen so he can cook me breakfast. I have to admit to being pleasantly surprised at his hidden talent. He slides a plate across the counter along with a glass of orange juice.

"Breakfast is served. Eat. I don't want you skipping meals."

I make a face at him but take a bite of my egg, cheese and tomato omelet. It's so good I can't contain a sigh of pleasure. He put a lot of cheese and just a touch of onions and it's divine. I don't even care that every one of these calories is likely to go straight to my hips. It's amazing what being around Finn even for a short time has done for my body image. He's always been vocal about telling me that he loves my body and that my curves make him hot. When I view myself through his eyes, I stop focusing on every little flaw and see the big picture. That he loves me just the way I am.

"You've picked up quite a few skills since the old days. I know you couldn't cook before," I tease.

"After I moved in here, I got tired of ordering in. It's been fun to experiment and try some different things. Tank's girlfriend gave me a few recipes to start off with. She's a pretty good cook."

"I can't wait to meet her. Any girl that can make your brother admit that he likes cuddling sounds like my kind of girl."

"Can you get some time off today?" Finn asks before he takes my plate and puts it in the dishwasher.

I think about it. One of our contracts is for a small boutique that's closed on Fridays. Tracy usually handles that one and she's mentioned to me before that she would love to get more hours. Usually it's only an issue because I prefer not to send the girls out to big contracts without supervision. But Tracy has been with us for almost two years and she's always been reliable. Maybe some of our staffing issues can be solved if I learn to trust a bit more.

"It's possible, why?"

"Because it's Friday night. I want to take my girl out on the town."

I can't suppress a little tremble of excitement. Going out on a proper date was something that we never got to do when we were younger. Finn and I worked part-time jobs to help our moms' with bills and we never really had extra money for that kind of thing anyway. Our dates were usually things you could do for free like hanging in the park or making out on the bleachers at school during football games.

"I guess we've never really done that, huh?"

Finn winks at me. "I can finally take you out properly. I always wanted to take you to one of those restaurants where they speak French and all the portion sizes look like they're for ants. You know, the real fancy places."

I think of all the proper, elegant dates I had with Andrew. The Carringtons have a lot of influence in the state and there were many dinners and fundraisers that Andy was expected to attend. All those evenings when I would try to fit my curves into a dress that his mother would find appropriate and then have to spend the evening smiling at the insipid people he was trying to impress. It seemed like he was always playing a role. Until the mask slipped and I saw the ugly underside.

Even when he took me out and we were alone, it never felt like I really had his full attention. Leaving him has gotten more of his attention than anything else I've ever done.

"I used to dream about that, too. But my dream wasn't about where we were going. It was just about having all that time with you. And you'd only have eyes for me."

"I only had eyes for you anyway," Finn replies.

"Now, I know that. But back then I'd see you flirting or smiling at someone else and it made me wonder. I wasn't sure if I was enough to keep a man like you interested."

117

It's difficult to admit out loud that my insecurity is what ultimately drove us apart. If only I'd trusted in him, we could have been together, loving each other, for all these years.

Finn looks pained. "I never knew that. I always thought of flirting as harmless. Half the time I don't even realize when I'm doing it. But it's obviously not harmless if it cost me you."

He looks so sad and that's not what I wanted at all.

"Okay, I'll make some calls and arrange for someone to cover for me tonight. Then I'll swing by my house and change clothes."

"Wear your best dress. And pack a bag before you come back." He gives me that intense stare again and my nerves start dancing again. Everything feels like it's moving so fast but I wouldn't stop it even if I could. For the first time, I'm doing something reckless and it feels completely right.

It feels like home.

* * * * *

When I get back to Finn's place that afternoon, I'm carrying a small suitcase and two garment bags. I brought one formal dress but also a really cute, black jersey knit dress that can pass for cocktail if necessary with the right accessories.

Finn hasn't told me anything about where we're going so I'm not sure which one I'm going to wear yet. I wish he'd give me a hint. Men don't understand these things. Being overdressed can be just as uncomfortable as being underdressed.

I'm in the tub again when he comes back home. I look up to see him observing me from the doorway.

"Another bath?"

Suddenly self-conscious about my obvious love for this decadent bathtub, I poke my tongue out at him. "I'm pampering myself before our date. I didn't get to relax last time. I was too busy being ravished by this insatiable caveman."

"Cavemen are so demanding, aren't they?" His eyes roam over every inch of my exposed skin. "I could definitely get used to this view."

I draw my knees up teasingly, blocking my breasts from his view. "You can't just watch me! If you want to see then you have to get in."

"If I get in there with you, we won't make dinner." But that doesn't stop him from sitting on the side of the tub and stroking his fingers over my skin.

"Hmm, are you sure?" Because I'm starting to care less and less about going out now that he's here and his hand is making its way slowly up my thigh.

"I'm sure. But that doesn't mean I can't play a little." His mouth covers mine just as his hand cups me. I arch into the touch and when I gasp, he chuckles against my mouth.

"So soft. So sweet. I could just play with this all day." He croons between kisses.

The water laps against the side of the tub as his arm moves, dancing over my pussy lips, teasing me until my hips lift of their own accord, trying to get more contact with his fingers. When I open my eyes, he's watching me. That sends my desire skyrocketing. I've never come like this, while I'm lost in ecstasy and he's so still. Watchful.

"I just want to see it. The moment when you fall apart. It's so beautiful."

Suddenly he thrusts one thick finger deep inside me, pressing and holding it there while his palm grinds against me. I explode against his hand, my cry swallowed when he kisses me again. The pleasure rolls through me like a wave until I'm leaning against Finn's arm completely boneless. When I open my eyes again, his carnal stare is fixed down at the water where his hand is buried between my thighs. He gently pulls his fingers out and I shudder at the small shocks of pleasure caused by the movement. He sees my reaction and grins, looking completely pleased with himself. I laugh weakly. I can't even fault the man for his arrogance in this particular case. He really is quite talented.

"This memory is going to keep me on the edge of my seat all night," he comments. He reaches for the towel and then extends his hand. I stand and step out of the tub, shivering as the cool air hits my skin. He rubs me briskly with the soft towel and then when I'm dry, tosses it on the floor. I just shake my head and bend over to pick it up and hang it back on the rack.

"Come on, we're going to be late."

"Late? Does that mean reservations?"

He chuckles at my attempt to pry our destination out of him. "Perhaps. But first we have a very important appointment."

I put on my best lingerie and at Finn's indication, the more formal dress. It's long and black with a sweetheart neckline that frames my chest perfectly.

When he sees me standing in front of the mirror, he pauses. "Every time I see you, I wonder how the hell I ever got so lucky."

The compliment sends a warm shiver through my veins. With a chest my size, it's hard to find dresses that don't make me look like a wannabe porn star but this one gives me a classic hourglass silhouette and I always feel beautiful when I wear it. Finn emerges from his closet a few minutes later wearing all black. A black suit, black shirt and a slim black tie. On anyone else it would probably look depressing but on him, the effect is magnetic.

"You look good, too. Very James Bond."

He laughs at that and then offers me his arm. When we walk out to the elevators together it all feels so magical. I want to giggle a little because I feel like I'm in a movie, getting whisked off for a night on the town with a handsome man.

The Bentley is at the curb and I smile at Jonah. He gives me the tight-lipped version of a smile that I've come to realize is just his way. I was sure he didn't like me in the beginning but then over time I observed that he's like this with everyone. He seems to take his job very seriously and I'm grateful for that.

It makes me feel better to know that Finn has someone watching his back. He worries about me but I worry the same way for him. Especially now that he has money because after my time in the Carringtons' world, I know just how many people are willing to lie, cheat, steal and even kill for it.

After we climb in, Finn gives Jonah a signal. I pout. I'd figured that I'd finally learn where we were going once we got in the car but it seems Finn has thought of that, too. My mind goes back to what he said earlier about having an appointment. I'm not sure what that even means but the excitement of not knowing has me practically bouncing in my seat.

Finn watches me squirm with an amused grin. "We're almost there, angel."

The car slows and turns. I peer out the window, reading the signs as we pass. Finally we pull into the driveway of a modest brick house.

"You're taking me to a house?" I look over at Finn. Then I realize where we are. "You're taking me to see Claire?"

"Yeah, I hope that's okay. She could really use the pick-me-up and I know she'll get a kick out of seeing us in our fancy clothes."

"Of course it's okay. I can't wait to see her again."

He opens the door with his key and ushers me into the living room. "Mom? We're here."

The house is cool and quiet. If I didn't know anyone was here, I would think it was empty. I glance over at Finn. I can feel the change come over him. I wish there was something I could do to help him but I don't know what. If my mother was sick, I'm not sure how I would handle it.

Finn squeezes my hand. "Have a seat. I'll just go make sure she's awake."

I nod. "Of course. And if she's not up for visitors, I completely understand."

He kisses my hand and then disappears into one of the bedrooms at the end of the hall. I walk to the couch and sit down to wait. A few minutes later, Finn leans his head back out. "She's ready now."

As soon as I walk into the bedroom, Claire lets out a little gasp. "Rissa Blake! Look at you. All grown up." Her voice is softer than I remember and she looks delicate. The scarf tied around her head makes her seem even smaller and fragile for some reason.

My heart breaks a little but I'm not here to remind her of how crappy she's been feeling. So with bravado that I don't really feel, I do a little twirl so she can see the full effect of the dress.

Claire claps and her smile widens. "You look so beautiful. Come here."

Dutifully, I approach and lean down to give her a hug. "It's really good to see you again, Claire. I was so sorry to hear about you being sick when Finn told me."

She glances over at her son. Finn has lowered himself to sit on the other side of the bed. I can tell that his leg must be bothering him again by the way he's got it stretched out. He never tells me when it's hurting but I'm starting to pick up on the signs.

"I can't believe Finn has been keeping you a secret all this time. I should have known there was something going on when he looked so happy the last few times he's visited. You always could make him laugh."

"He makes me laugh, too. And drives me crazy. He tells me to get dressed up but won't tell me where we're going!"

She looks over at Finn. "That sounds like him. But you both look wonderful. I love the neckline on this dress, too."

Fashion was always one of the ways Claire and I connected. She'd welcomed me with open arms and declared that now she had someone to talk about "girl things" with. I know Finn and Tank both used to complain that their Mom would tell them stories with way too much romantic detail in them. But I personally loved hearing her stories. Claire was always animated and fun, a lot like my mom.

Funny how I never realized how much I missed this, being a part of Finn's family until now.

"I know my mom would love to come visit you sometimes, too."

Claire reaches out for my hand. "Oh that would be wonderful. Gloria was always a lot of fun. You kids don't even know some of the fun we got into when you weren't around. Two hot mamas on the prowl!"

Finn groans and I can't contain my laughter. "Gloria is still on the prowl. I'm sure she'll tell you all about her newest boyfriend."

We chat for a little bit longer and I give her mom's cell phone number since I know my mom won't mind.

After about half an hour, Finn glances at his watch. "Well, I guess we'd better get going."

He leans down and kisses Claire's cheek. I do the same.

"We'll let you get some sleep now, Mom."

"Thank you for coming by. Now take this beautiful girl out and show her a good time." Claire's eyes are already drooping so I know it's definitely time for us to leave.

As we walk back down the driveway to the car, Finn suddenly pulls me into his arms. "Thank you."

"For what?"

"Making her smile. For making me laugh. For being you."

The tears I made myself tamp down in front of Claire spring to my eyes again. The reality that Claire might not recover scares me. Because Finn has already had to deal with so much tragedy in his life. "I really hope she gets better."

"Me too. Now come on. I have something else I want to show you."

Chapter Nine

Finn

A week later, Jonah drops me off in front of the StarCrest hotel. It's time for another one of my scheduled visits with my father. After spending the past week with Rissa, it's hard to get back to the real world. Time seems to suspend when we're together. After visiting my mom, I'd taken her to the most expensive, most exclusive restaurant in the area. We'd spent about ten minutes admiring the beautiful atmosphere and sipping champagne.

Then she'd leaned across the table and told me proper dates were boring and she'd really rather I took her home and fucked her in the Jacuzzi again. I left five hundred dollars on the table and didn't bother waiting for the check.

Ever since then she's been delegating more of her work and spending more time at home. We've been encapsulated in a glorious little bubble, isolated away from everything except the way we feel about each other.

But there are certain obligations that can't be neglected. My father definitely falls into that category.

When I first learned of my newfound inheritance, I was surprised to find out that my father owns a large amount of local real estate. Not just hotels but restaurants and businesses. Considering that he left us alone to fend for ourselves for the better part of two decades, it was a shock to learn that he'd never really left the area. He's been investing heavily in Virginia for the majority of his life.

I walk slowly through the lobby to the elevators, cursing the need to use my cane. Some days I can leave it behind but when walking on these slick polished floors, I need the stability. As I step into the elevator, I ignore the blatant stares and pitying glances from the other people on board. A young man with a cane is always a sight, no matter how hard people try not to notice.

Finally I'm the last one and the elevator dings as I reach Max's floor. The petite redhead who answers his door smiles brightly at me. "Finn, come in. He's waiting for you."

"Thank you, darling."

Rissa's words about my flirting come back to me. Flirting comes naturally to me and I never think about it as anything serious. But hearing from Rissa that my behavior played a part in the way things worked out made an impression on me.

I follow her into the living room of the suite. My father is already there, his wheelchair positioned next to the window. I know he hates being in it just as I hate using my cane. But since he's fresh out of the hospital after a heart attack, he should be happy just to be home.

"Finn. Come in."

I move to the couch facing him and lower myself carefully, stretching my leg out. These weekly meetings are basically bullshit but they make my bank account happy so I show up every week. I got a reprieve for the last few weeks since Max was fresh out of the hospital and still recovering. We all visited him while he was there multiple times and that seemed to make him happy.

"They won't bring me a burger. I should fire them all. Start over." Max grumbles.

I stifle a smile. He looks so disgruntled, like a child who's been denied his favorite toy. Then I imagine the juicy burger his chef prepared for me the last time I was here. Maybe he's not entirely unjustified in his desire. I could easily get spoiled eating like that.

"You won't be firing anyone today, Max. Just relax." The redhead smiles down at him affectionately which seems to settle him down a little. That's one thing I've noticed about my father, he seems to inspire a great deal of loyalty in most of his staff members. I'm assuming he's probably paying them pretty well.

"I saw Luke." I don't mention that I've been visiting him every other day.

Max immediately perks up. "You did? What did he say?"

"I don't think you want me to repeat some of what he said."

He wheels himself to the sideboard and pours himself a drink. He holds up the bottle to me and I shake my head.

"Luke thinks you're hiding something."

His hand pauses in mid-pour and some of the liquid sloshes over the side of the glass. "What do you mean?"

"That's why he doesn't want to see you. He thinks you're up to something. That there's a good reason that I should stay away from you. Is he right?"

Max pours a little more in the glass before he turns to face me. "Probably. Does that mean you're going to stop coming?"

This is the first time he's acknowledged any wrongdoing. Even though it's a small concession, it makes me feel better anyway.

"No, I'm not going to stop coming."

For a moment, his eyes flash with joy and then he turns back to his drink. This seems to be an obsession of his, getting all of his children back together, making contact with all of us. Not that it's not a fine sentiment but I can't help but wonder why it matters to him so much. It's been years and all of our lives have been progressing just fine. Why the sudden need for a family reunion? Why the urgency?

"Whatever it is, you might as well just tell us. It'll come out in the end anyway so why fight it?"

He grunts. "Only young people think that way. We older folk know there's something to timing. To waiting for the perfect moment."

129

"I'm not sure I believe perfect exists anymore."

All I can think of is Rissa's face this morning. She'd looked so right in my bed, as close to perfect as I think exists in this world. The first time I loved her, I would have done anything, given anything for her. I've had her on a pedestal in my mind for all the wrong reasons. Both of us have used time to twist our memories and only focused on the good things. We'd dreamed of so much together, building a home, filling it with kids someday. But that's all they were. Dreams.

None of those dreams took into account our very real flaws and the inevitable pitfalls of just living life. Maybe it was because we were so young or maybe it was just our destiny to walk away from each other before we could find our way back. But I've come to the understanding that just because things weren't perfect between us doesn't mean that they were wrong.

Or maybe that's what perfect really means in this world. Seeing the flaws in someone yet loving them anyway.

My father is struggling to reconnect with the people in his life after manipulating and lying to them. I don't want to end up like that. I pull out my phone and quickly compose an email to Patrick Stevens.

Patrick,

My plans have changed. Put all company acquisitions on hold until further notice.

I send the message and then look up to see Max watching me. His eyes narrow. "I see a lot of me in you."

"I'm nothing like you, Max."

His eyes glaze over slightly and I move forward, worried that he's having another attack.

"Max? Are you okay?"

He nods quickly. "Just short of breath sometimes. This old body is failing me. And I don't have the time to right all the wrongs I've done. I've done bad things, Finn. Hurt people. Mainly people who loved me. I'm just trying to make it right."

"Some things can't be fixed that easily."

Max watches me with sad eyes. "I know. But we can try."

*　*　*　*　*

After I leave my father, I head over to the hospital. Mom was scheduled to have another procedure this morning but she assured me it was nothing serious. I would have rescheduled my time with Max anyway if Tank hadn't told me he would be there with her. He already texted me her room number.

Having Rissa at my place in the mornings has altered my schedule slightly. I smile wondering if Mom has figured out that Rissa is practically living with me yet. Usually she's on top of these things. She's always noticed everything, especially when it's something I'm trying to hide.

My smile fades as soon as I enter her room and see the look on her face. Something is wrong.

"I'll be back later when we get the latest test results." Dr. Singh, her oncologist, nods at me before leaving the room.

Mom smiles brightly when she sees me. "Finn. I told you, you really don't have to come every time I'm scheduled for a procedure."

Suddenly she claps a hand over her mouth. The action doesn't cover her soft cry. She takes another deep breath in and out. Then she squeezes her eyes shut and tears spill over her cheeks and onto her hand.

"Mom?" I rush to her side and sit awkwardly on the edge of the bed. She grabs my arm and that sends a cold shaft of fear arrowing straight through my heart. Throughout this entire process, she's been steady and positive. No matter how much comfort I've offered, she's always seemed as though she doesn't need it. I knew it was because she just didn't want me to see her cry. But the way she's holding on to me now means she's too distraught to hide it anymore.

Eventually her sobs slow and then taper off until she manages to catch her breath. Her fingers unfurl from the sleeves of my shirt and she raises her head. When our eyes meet, she manages a shaky smile. "I'm glad you're here, Finn."

"Me too." There's really nothing else I can say. I have no idea how to process what's just happened.

Mom pulls the sheet on the bed higher, looking like she wishes she could disappear behind it. For once, the television isn't playing in the background and the silence swells around us. The mindless shows that usually annoy me make more sense now. Noise and activity of any kind is preferable to this awful silence.

"What happened?" I ask after she's gotten herself under control.

She sighs. "It didn't work. The new treatment. It appears to have had no effect at all."

I sit as close to her as I possibly can with the guardrail of the bed in the way. "I'm so sorry. So sorry." There's really nothing else I can say and that helplessness tears at me. This treatment was supposed to be our miracle. It was supposed to make her better.

She pulls me down for a hug. Then she pulls back and pats at the wet spot on my shirt. "I'm so sorry. I shouldn't be putting this all on you."

"Mom, this is about *you*. You should cry or whatever you need to do."

I have to squeeze my own eyes hard to stop the tears. She doesn't need to see me break down. My mom has always been the strong one, even when she had no one to rely on but herself. Now she needs me to be strong for her.

"I'm going to have a talk with the doctor. They said we have other options. Treatments that are overseas. We're not giving up."

By now, she seems to have gotten herself under control. She wipes the back of her eyes with a tissue and forces a tremulous smile. "I know. Maybe that won't be so bad. I've always wanted to travel."

"Switzerland is nice this time of year."

Her breath huffs out in a little laugh. "Yes, I suppose it is."

"Can I come in?"

We look up to see Emma standing in the doorway. Tank stands behind her, stone-faced.

"Of course, sweetheart. Please." Mom opens her arms and Emma practically flies across the room to hug her.

Tank told me a little about Emma's background so I know she

lost her parents violently. It explains why she's so attached to our mom. I can't even imagine a world where I don't have my mother to nag me, tease me and build me up. I don't want to either.

"I need to talk to you."

Tank nods and follows me outside. My brother and I are very different, but when it comes to our mother we've always been in perfect agreement. We'll work together to get anything she needs. And he's not going to take the news any better than I have.

"So it didn't work."

We'd paid to try out an experimental form of chemotherapy that isn't usually offered. I paid to fly the foremost oncologist who pioneered the treatment here so that he could oversee her care. At the time, it seemed like our best option.

Tank's hands flex into fists and I know he feels the same restless rage that torments me. We're men of action. When there's a problem, we need to fix it. But this battle isn't one that we can fight for her.

"There has to be something else," he mutters.

"If there is, we'll find out."

He glances behind me at Mom's open door. A nurse has just gone in to take more blood or her temperature or one of the million things they constantly seem to be doing. It hits me then that all this might be for nothing. The futility hits me hard.

This might be a battle that we just can't win.

* * * * *

The beep beep of the machine next to my mother's bed slips into my dreams. I wake with the sound echoing in my head. Mom is fast asleep, looking altogether too pale against the stark sheets. I glance at my watch. It's almost midnight. I can't believe the nurses didn't kick me out by now. Visiting hours have long since been over. I need to get home before Rissa gets back from her last shift or she'll be worried.

I stand and kiss Mom gently on the forehead, then pick up my cane. When I emerge into the bright light of the hospital corridor, I almost collide with Sandy.

"Sorry. I should have been gone hours ago. I guess I fell asleep."

"It's perfectly all right. Honestly, I didn't have the heart to wake you." She glances toward Mom's room. "We're all very fond of her."

I nod because I don't trust myself to speak.

When I get home, I go straight to my room and strip. Sleeping in that chair has left my neck tight and my back sore. A hot shower is probably what I need but I'm too tired to trust myself not to fall out in the shower. Rissa still hasn't arrived home and for once, I'm actually glad for the privacy.

I shake out several pills, then at the last minute shake out a few more. The pills roll around my palm making little clacking noises and I shake them gently, just to hear the sound. There's a sick sense of excitement just looking at them. I know that they're going to make me feel good.

Ashamed at the thought, I close my hand.

The past week, I've been dealing with the pain unmedicated. I need a break. Just a few hours without the cloud of pain. I need a few moments when things don't have to make sense. When I can remember a time when my mom was smiling and when I didn't have to watch her in pain.

When loving so much didn't hurt.

Before I can think about it too hard, I toss back the handful of pills. I fill the glass on the counter with water and wash them down.

I climb into the bed and fall face forward into the pillows. Rissa will be home soon but by the time we wake up tomorrow morning, I'll be fine.

The next thing I know, there's noise all around me. It feels like waking up in a blender.

I struggle to make my groggy limbs respond. Everything feels heavy like I have little anvils attached to my arms and legs.

When I finally get on my feet, I stumble into the hallway. Colors swirl around me and the hallways shifts and rolls beneath my feet. Why is everything moving? I just want it to be still, the way it's supposed to be.

I look up and then I see Marissa. Just like I always dreamed standing in a field of flowers.

"You should always be surrounded by roses. If I'd had the money to, I would have bought you some everyday."

Her eyes smile at me, dancing around her head in circles before settling above her cheeks again. "Finn, what are you talking about? Was I making too much noise? I was trying not to wake you up."

Her words don't make sense to me. Nothing makes sense to me anymore. The woman who has loved me all my life is sick and nothing I've tried has saved her. The woman I've hated is here in front of me and yet still out of reach. She won't tell me she loves me. She won't move in. She won't be mine.

"Why are you here? You don't want me. You never wanted me."

She moves closer and then suddenly she's right in front of me. "I wanted you, Finn. I've always wanted you. That's why I'm here."

Seeing her was just another form of torture. She was just one more person who hadn't thought I was worth anything. The girl who left me for a man who could give her all the pretty shiny things she wanted.

"You didn't always want me. You wanted *him*. How did that work out for you, angel? Did he buy you whatever you wanted? Could he give you all those gifts that I couldn't afford?"

She's watching me with those sad eyes. Those eyes that remind me of all my flaws. It makes me angry.

"And now I'm here, rich as fuck and I can't even enjoy it because you're still here. I hate you and I want you. Why can't you just get out of my head?"

The pressure behind my forehead is enormous. I press my hands on both sides of my temples and squeeze. Maybe if I push hard enough I can crush all the dark thoughts. But when I open my eyes, she's still there. This demon that looks like the woman I loved.

"Just get out of my head!" I scream and keep going until everything goes dark.

Chapter Ten

Rissa

I race out of the building, ignoring John's concerned call. Tears are streaming from my eyes so fast that I can barely see but somehow I find my way to where my car is parked on the street. With shaking fingers I hit the button to unlock it. Once I'm inside, I just sit there willing my heart to stop beating so fast.

I'm not even sure what just happened. Rain pounds the windshield and the sound is comforting. It feels like the rain is insulating me against the outside world. That's what I need, something to act as a buffer until I can get my equilibrium back. Whatever that was ... I think back to what just happened upstairs.

I'm not even sure what to call that, a rage? I've never seen Finn like that before. He didn't even look like he was in his right mind.

And the things he was saying. As bad as the raw physical violence I'd sensed in him was, the vile, mean things spilling from his lips were even worse.

Finn is the last person that I ever thought I'd have to be afraid of.

After a few minutes my pulse rate has slowed a bit so I turn on the car and pull out into the road. There's a loud screech and then a horn blares on my left. Just like that my heart is back in my throat as I look over at the truck that almost smashed into my side.

The man behind the wheel makes an angry gesture and then speeds off. I'm too shaken to pull out right then so I wait a few minutes with my head on the steering wheel. Then I look both ways carefully and make a turn in the opposite direction.

At first my thoughts were just go home but that's not what I need right now. I don't want to sit alone in my house worrying that Andrew might show up. I could go to my mom's house but she'll ask too many questions, things I'm not ready to talk about yet. Right now I just need my girls.

I arrive at the office and let out a small sigh of relief to see the lights are on. Someone is here.

As soon as I walk in, Daphne looks up. Her mouth forms an O. "What happened to you?"

I look down. It's only then I realize that I've walked through the rain and am now dripping on the floor, my hair plastered to my head.

"Finn … I had to get out of there."

Daphne jumps up and helps me to her chair. I sit, shivering while she bustles around me. She produces a sweatshirt from somewhere and helps me pull my soaking wet T-shirt over my head. Once I have the warm sweatshirt on, she leaves briefly to bring me a cup of tea. When she returns, Tara is with her.

"What did he do?"

"He was screaming at me and he was so angry. I've never seen him like that." I take a sip of the hot tea and the warmth slides down my throat and spreads through me.

"I knew we should have refused that contract. Who the hell does he think he is?"

"Tara, he was so angry. I just can't go back there. Not again." Our eyes meet and I know she understands that I'm talking about a lot more than a cleaning contract. I raise my hand to my head, feeling through my hair to the raised scar a few inches back from my temple. I threw away years of my life thinking that if I just held on, if I just forgave Andy one more time that things would be better. I can't go back to that. Not for anyone.

Not even for Finn.

Her eyes linger on my damp hair. "We need to get you home, honey." She helps me out of the chair and Daphne follows behind us. She locks the door as we leave. Then I realize what time it is. It's early morning and they both have clients. In fact, they're both late.

"You guys don't have to babysit me. I know we're stretched thin. You can go and we'll talk this evening."

"Oh no. We're not leaving you alone. As soon as Daphne told me what happened, I called Tracy to cover for me."

"And I was scheduled to do some paperwork this morning anyway," Daphne chimes in. "So it's fine. It's more important that we take care of you right now."

Tara holds up her cell phone. "Cooperate or I'm calling your Mom."

*   *   *   *   *

I cuddle up on my couch while Daphne and Tara pace the floor. As soon as we arrived, they ushered me into my room to clean up. When I saw my face in the mirror I almost scared myself. Half of my hair was sticking up on the side and my eyes look hollow and gaunt in my face.

"Bastard!"

"Jerk!"

"Neanderthal!"

The insults fly back and forth as they take turns cursing Finn up one side and down the other. Daphne in particular is really getting into it. She rarely curses and never has a harsh word for anyone so I'm surprised to see her so furious. I think she must have some residual frustration built up from over the years that is finally finding an outlet.

"We should sue his ass." That was Tara. I was surprised she hadn't mentioned it before now. Daphne is hurt on my behalf but Tara, she's pissed. I can see it in her tense stance and the way her eyes keep darting back and forth. Her sharp mind is looking for some way out of this situation. She wants to do more than just curse Finn's name. She wants to go after him. She wants blood.

"The contract states that all disputes must go through arbitration."

Tara growls at that. "That damn contract. He's a snake but he's a smart snake. That's a scary combination."

Daphne finally abandons her pacing and sits next to me on the couch. I lean over and cuddle against her. She strokes my hair.

"I still can't believe that he did this. He seemed so nice that day. Now I wish I'd kicked him in the balls while he was standing in front of me." Daphne seems to be taking it hard that she didn't see through Finn's charm. I already told her that she's in good company. There aren't many women who are immune to Finn.

"Are you upset that I didn't tell you about our past?" She hasn't said anything or done anything that makes me think she's mad at me but in her position, I would be a little hurt. After all, I confided the whole story to Tara right away and deliberately kept Daphne in the dark.

Daphne shakes her head. "It's your story to tell. You shouldn't have to share it with anyone if you don't want to. I just hope you don't think that I would have judged you."

"No, that was honestly the last thing I thought." I struggle to find the words to explain. "It's just that you guys know this version of me. The one who has herself together. That girl that I was before, well I like to leave her in the past."

Daphne leans back and tucks her feet beneath her. "I understand that."

The doorbell rings and I immediately tense. I took a risk coming back here knowing that Andrew has been sniffing around. I glance over at Tara. "Can you get rid of whoever that is? And if it's Andrew, I'm calling the cops."

Tara looks slightly guilty. "It's not Andrew." She jumps up and walks to the door. After peering out of the peephole, she pulls the door open. My mom sweeps in with her arms outstretched. "There's my baby. What did he do to you?"

Normally my mother's interference would drive me crazy but right here and now, I find that she's exactly what I need. She sits on the couch next to me and when she opens her arms again, I lean into her embrace.

She wipes away my tears with her thumb and then squeezes my shoulders. "Let's get you into bed, sweetie."

"Okay." The events of the morning are catching up with me and I let out a huge yawn. Being tucked into bed by my mother actually sounds like heaven.

The girls walk ahead into my room. Daphne turns back the covers and I slip beneath fully dressed. I can't seem to get warm enough. Mom tucks my covers beneath my chin the same way she used to do when I was a child.

"Go to sleep, sweetie. It'll all look better after you've had some rest."

* * * * *

I wake up a few hours later. Mom is still downstairs but the girls left. Slowly the whole story comes out and she holds me as I sob. She doesn't say anything or offer any advice but just tells me to get my things.

"I don't want you staying here alone."

Even though I really want to stay in my own bed, I agree that it would not be a good thing if Andy were to show up here when I'm in this frame of mind. It took everything I had to stand up to him the last time and part of me knows that I'm not that brave. I was only able to do that because I knew Finn was there. So I pack a bag and we ride over to my mom's modest three-bedroom rancher.

She ushers me into the second bedroom right across the hall from her room. When I helped her buy the house, we decorated this room with my favorite colors, soft lavender with hints of yellow in all the accent pillows. It's a very cheerful room and even though I didn't grow up in this house, my mom's warm presence makes it feel like home anyway.

"I'm sure you just want some time alone to think but I just want to say this sweetie. I never liked Andrew. He's one of them *my-shit-don't-stink* types. But Finn, he was always a good boy. I don't know what's going on with him but I think we should find out."

"I wish I'd listened to you about Andy."

"Well, I hope I'm right about Finn this time. He was a sweet one and boy was he stuck on you."

After she leaves, I sit on the edge of the bed. Suddenly it seems so

144

quiet. I've never had an issue being alone before but seeing Finn like that has left me shaken.

After double-checking the locks on the front and back door, I slip into the bathroom and remove my clothes. I run the water as hot as I can stand it and then get in. The steam curls up all around me and I rest my head on the ledge of the tub. My eyes close and I let the tears flow.

What happened between us? Where did things go so wrong? It feels like a double betrayal because after how awful he was to me in the beginning, over the last few weeks he's been so different. The man who helped me clean and waited outside just so I wouldn't have to walk to my car alone at night cannot be the same man who just terrified me.

I look at the faint white lines on the back of my arm. Andrew hadn't liked the way I was talking to one of his colleagues at his company Christmas party. When we got home that night, he backhanded me so hard that I fell into a glass table.

I cringe thinking about that time in my life. Things were never great between us but that had marked a turning point when I could no longer rationalize the things he did and said to me. The ways he put me down and tried to undermine my confidence.

Tonight, for the first time in years I felt completely helpless all over again. Finn has taken away my sense of safety and that's not something I can easily forgive him for.

Chapter Eleven

Finn

When you love something, it has power over you. I knew Rissa had me by the balls but I never knew how tight her grip was until she didn't come home.

"Yes, I know she's not at work today. I'm asking if anyone there can tell me why. Has she called?"

"Sir, we can't give out that kind of information."

"I know you can't give out information about her but I'm just asking if anyone there has actually talked to her today."

I let out a groan when the person on the other end hangs up. "*Damn it.*" The people at her company are just doing their jobs but that's little consolation when she could be hurt somewhere. Alone and scared.

Fear makes my chest so tight I almost can't breathe. If something happened to her, no one would even know to notify me. After driving by her house and looking in the windows, I'd eventually given up and come back here. Her car was still parked on the street outside of her office. It was like she'd gone to work and then vanished into thin air.

I pull out my phone again. "Jonah, I need the car."

I walk into my office and then pull out the file Patrick Stevens assembled on Rissa last month. I'd asked him to find out everything about her which was why I had information about her business partners. But there was one person that would always know how to find her.

I run my finger down the page until I find the address for Gloria Blake. Then I take the elevator down to the first floor. By the time I walk out of the building, Jonah is just pulling up to the curb. I get in and tell him the address.

When we pull up, I recognize Daphne's sporty little green car. Rissa must be here.

I look at Jonah. "I'm not sure exactly what I'm walking into so this may take a while."

He nods. "Of course, sir."

I climb out and then walk up the driveway. The front beds are planted with cheerful pansies that add wild splashes of color to the otherwise plain yard. I knock on the door and then step back to wait.

The door swings open.

"You have some nerve showing up here."

The brunette standing in Rissa's doorway glares at me. The effect is ruined slightly by the cheerful blue streaks running down the side of her head.

"You must be Tara." She's the opposite of Rissa's other business partner. This one looks like a lioness ready to take down her prey. And she's looking at me like she's more than ready to sink her teeth in.

"Yes, I am. I don't need you to introduce yourself. You're just the asshole who scared my friend out of her mind this morning."

Her words shed a little light on why Rissa has suddenly gone MIA. But how could I have scared her when I haven't even seen her?

"What are you talking about? I'm here because Rissa didn't come home last night. I called your office and they won't tell me anything. I was worried."

"Worried? You're the reason my friend is currently buried under the blankets and scared of the world right now. She said you screamed at her. That you scared her!"

I take a step back, the jumbled memories of that night are starting to make sense. The weird dream I had about Rissa must have been real. Or at least some of it. I don't even remember everything just seeing flowers and feeling like my head was going to pop off. And screaming.

Oh god. She saw me like that.

Suddenly Daphne appears over her shoulder. "I thought you

were a nice guy! I would have never told you where Rissa was that day if I'd known you would do this."

It's a powerful thing to see them both ready to take me down in defense of their friend. One looks determined and the other looks scared to death. Only someone as strong and resolute as Rissa could demand this kind of loyalty just by existing.

"I know this looks bad, hell it is bad, but it's not what you think. I would never scare Rissa on purpose."

Tara comes out on the porch and slams the screen behind her. "That may be true but it doesn't change the fact that Rissa was crying. That doesn't happen often. So, I don't give a damn how much money you have and I don't care if you kill our contract. She's been through too much already and no one is going to put her through this hell again."

"Again? Someone scared her before?" I think back to the night Andrew was waiting at her house and suddenly the whole scene makes a lot more sense. It also makes me so angry that I'm not sure I trust myself to even speak. "Please, just tell Rissa I'm here," I whisper.

"Why do you even care? You've obviously just been stringing her along. Otherwise, why would you invite her to stay with you and then scream at her to get out when she comes back?"

With a defeated sigh, I sit down on the step. "There's a whole story behind this but that story is for Rissa alone. I know you're trying to protect her and I'm glad she has you guys."

That seems to take some of the fun out of it for Tara. She scowls and then says, "Well, don't go getting all sentimental now. I'm having too much fun yelling at you."

I'm starting to understand why she's friends with Rissa. They have the same sarcastic sense of humor.

"You can watch us from the window while I talk to her and then I'll be out of your hair. But you don't have to worry. I've spent the past few hours in hell thinking that something happened to her. I love her more than I knew it was possible to love. And all I want is the chance to explain."

* * * * *

They leave me sitting out there for ten minutes before the door opens again. Gloria steps out on the porch and I immediately get to my feet.

"Miss Blake. It's nice to see you again."

Gloria looks at me for a long moment. "What's going on with you, young man?"

I didn't want to give this information out to just anyone but I'm incapable of lying when Rissa's mother is asking me to explain myself.

"I'm on heavy pain medication, ma'am. I thought I was dreaming."

She nods thoughtfully then opens her arms to me for a hug. "I'm glad I didn't misjudge you. You were always a good one. Come on in here then."

I enter the house and then take a seat on the couch.

"I'll go get Rissa." Gloria smiles kindly at me and then walks down the hallway and out of sight.

Now that I know Rissa is coming, I'm hit with a sudden case of nerves. I have to explain my erratic behavior and ask for her forgiveness. And there's no guarantee that she'll give it.

Rissa finally appears in the doorway. With no makeup and her wild curls pulled off her face, she looks so young.

There's so much of the girl I loved still in her face. But for the first time I'm noticing all the ways she's different. In some ways more fragile and in other ways stronger. I didn't think it was possible but the love I feel for the woman she's become makes the way I felt about the girl look like a crush. My first instinct is to protect her at all costs. I want to make sure that no one ever hurts her again, including me.

She sits on the other end of the couch. "I heard you were calling the office looking for me. I don't know why."

"That's because you have no idea how worried I was when I woke up this morning and you weren't there."

She shakes her head. "But I was there. I got up to get ready for work and then you came out to the living room talking about buying me flowers. You were screaming at me."

"I don't remember any of that."

"What was wrong with you? I've never seen you like that."

"Drugs do that to you."

"You're not ..."

"A druggie? Yeah, I am. The pain pills that keep me sane also cause me to hallucinate sometimes. I've been hiding it from everyone around me. But just like always, you see the things no one else does."

It's humiliating to bare myself like this to her. I would love to be able to stay a hero in her eyes but she's always been the one person that I couldn't keep a secret from. So my worst moments will always be played out in front of the person I most want to impress.

"I know I scared you and there are no words that can explain how shitty that makes me feel. I only came here to make sure that you're okay. And to tell you that you don't have to worry about me bothering you anymore."

"What?" She turns and looks at me, her blue eyes going wide.

"I'm not good for you. And you were right to run away from me." I stand and Rissa jumps up as well.

"This entire time, you've been saying that this whole thing is unhealthy and I shouldn't be trying to hang on to the past. You're getting your wish. I'm terminating the contract effective immediately. I'll pay out the remaining balance for the next six months anyway since the breach is on my side."

I can't resist pulling her into my arms and kissing her forehead. She grabs onto the front of my shirt, hanging fast even as I'm trying to pull away.

"Goodbye, Rissa."

I wave to Gloria, who stands watching us from the hallway. Once I get outside on the porch, I take in a deep lungful of air, feeling like I suddenly can't breathe.

Every step I take away from the house seems to require more and more effort. Jonah is still parked alongside the curb and when he sees me, he starts the car.

No more revenge, no more uncertainty, no more jealousy. No more Rissa. Things will go back to the way they were.

Just before I get to the car, the screen door bangs open behind me. I turn to see Rissa running across the lawn. She stops right in front of me and pokes me in the chest with her finger.

"You know how I feel about charity. I'll do the work that I'm getting paid for. But what happened yesterday, that can never happen again."

Hope blooms inside my chest. Then I squash it just as quickly. Even if Rissa is willing to forgive me, there's something I need to do first before we can be together. Right now, I'm a risk factor and she doesn't need another one of those in her life.

Which means that I'll have to leave her for a little while.

"Did you hear me?" She gives me that sassy look I love and then pokes me again. "You scared me, Finn. I can't be scared like that anymore."

"It will never happen again. You have my word on that. I'll see you tomorrow." I turn to go before she has a chance to change her mind.

"What do you mean tomorrow? I haven't done my work for today so I'll see you there in an hour."

She turns and runs back to the house. I get in the car with a big grin on my face. Even though I know I have to leave her, I plan on enjoying all the time with her I can get before then.

* * * * *

When Rissa opens the door, she's so overladen with bags that she doesn't even see me at first. She's wearing jeans and a soft lemon colored sweater. Her wild red curls are still bound up in that messy knot on top of her head that instantly makes me want to pull it down.

And in that moment, my heart speeds up and my whole body seems to sing. Just seeing her makes me happy but I try to tamp down my reaction. Things are still precarious after what happened this morning and I don't want to drive her away.

Just the thought makes me feel weak. I've had years to plan the things I would say to her, how I'd make her regret leaving me. But in all my planning the one thing I didn't plan on was falling for her again.

And now I'm caught up in her spell, just like a teenage boy with a crush.

When Rissa finally drops the mess of bags she's holding, she looks over to the kitchen. When she finally notices me, she lets out a little squeak of surprise.

"Finn! Were you waiting on me to get here?" The subtle pink in her cheeks betrays that she's not entirely comfortable being around me just yet.

"I wanted to catch you before you started. I need you downstairs today."

She grabs her supplies and follows behind dutifully as I walk out into the hallway and then lock up behind us.

"What do you need me to do downstairs?"

"I need you to do a final clean on Apartment 2A."

"Oh." She falls silent and then looks over at me again. "Any reason?"

"The building manager called and asked if we could change the move-in date for a certain tenant. He'll be moving in tonight."

We get on the elevator and ride down to the second floor. "I've designated this floor for everyone with disabilities because there is a ramp going down to the first floor. I don't want anyone trapped in the event of an emergency."

"That's smart."

I open the door to the unit with my key and usher her in. "It just needs a last minute check to make sure it's presentable. The tenant should be here soon."

She walks around the room, and then leans down to peer closely at the counters. "This looks like it was just cleaned."

Was it? I think back over the schedule she'd shown me for the last week. I must have gotten the units mixed up. Not that it really matters since I was just using this last minute cleaning as an excuse.

Rissa frowns at me then disappears into the back of the unit. She goes into each bedroom and then comes back out into the hall. I avoid her eyes and eventually she disappears into the bathroom. When she comes back out, she crosses her arms. "This place is completely clean. Why are we really here?"

The doorbell rings. Rissa jumps and looks around.

I let out a sigh of relief, grateful for the interruption. "The new tenant must be here."

I open the door and usher the two men on the other side in. One is the building manager I hired a few months ago and the other must be the newest tenant. As he passes, his gait is only slightly uneven. I would never know he wears a prosthesis if I hadn't read his file.

The building manager shakes my hand and then introduces us. After assuring him that I'll take things from here, I turn back to my newest tenant.

"Rissa, I'd like to introduce Major Clark Halliwell. Major, this is Marissa Blake. She works here getting the apartments ready for move-in."

He shakes her hand. "Well, I can see you've done a great job."

Rissa beams at the compliment. "Thank you. Welcome to the building."

While the other man walks around and explores the apartment, Rissa comes up at my elbow. "Did you do this just so I don't have to come up to your place again?"

I don't even have to answer that question. She's always been clever so I don't try to pretend. "You should never have to be afraid, Rissa."

Major Halliwell turns from where he stands at the window. "I want to thank you for this Mr. Marshall. This is much more than I was expecting."

I switch my cane to my left hand and extend my right hand to shake. "No, thank you for your years of service. We'll leave now so you can get settled."

Rissa follows me out into the hallway. We walk in companionable silence. As we pass one of the other units, she pokes her head in to check on her crew.

"They've made a lot of progress," I remark. And they have. I never could have guessed when I hired Rissa that this entire floor would be ready so fast.

"Yeah, they have. I have some of the best crews out there. I always choose the ones that really want it. The ones that others turn down because they have a disability or because they have children. So many people think that these things slow you down on the job but those same things also make my crew more determined. I remember how hard it was for my mom. She got fired from so many jobs because she needed to be there for me when I got sick. I promised myself that one day I would be the boss and that I would never be like that."

We get on the elevator and I push the button for the lobby. "I can see what kind of boss you are. You're amazing."

She waves the compliment away. "We all cover for each other when needed."

Once the elevator stops moving, she peers at the elevator panel, as if just realizing that we've gone down instead of up. "Aren't we going back to your place? I still haven't cleaned."

I shake my head. "You don't need to. We both know that wasn't why I hired you."

She doesn't exit the elevator so I sigh and walk out into the lobby. If she won't leave then I will. I can hear her shoes squeaking on the floor as she hurries behind me.

"Mr. Stevens originally told me that the entire building had gone through a recent upgrade and redesign. I assumed the owner was planning to sell the building not keep it. But there's no way normal people could afford this kind of real estate."

"You're right. The people who most deserve these apartments can't afford them. Not without a little help, anyway."

"That's why you've been renovating this building. You're donating all these apartments?" She turns to me, her eyes bright. "That's why you insisted that we concentrate on one floor at a time. You've been lining up tenants and scheduling them to move in."

"Not all of them will be donated but at least a third. I know what it's like to leave the military and wonder if you can make it."

"That's really nice of you."

I grunt at that. "I'm not a nice guy. Don't fool yourself. I brought you here to get payback for how you left me. My plan was to hurt you and I succeeded. I'm not a nice guy. I'm an asshole."

She shakes her head. "Don't try to make it seem like you were just pretending this whole time. I know you and you meant every single thing you said to me. You love me."

It would be kinder to just lie to her. To pretend that this was all part of my plan from the beginning and to make her hate me. Then she could go on with her life without a backward glance. But when I look over at her, her eyes glow with knowledge. She smiles like she knows what I'm about to do and is already amused by it.

She always sees everything.

"You're right. I meant every word. That doesn't mean that I'm good for you though. We need to slow down and I definitely need to figure my shit out. Because I can't take the chance that I'll ever scare you like that again. Or that I might hurt you. I'm more determined now but I'm also more cautious. I'm not as reckless as I used to be because I know now how much I have to lose."

"You told me that you weren't going to let me go so easily this time. Was that a lie, too?"

Now that bothers me so I take her by the arm and pull her over to the small lobby area so we aren't giving the concierge such a show. "I wasn't lying. I've never lied to you. I'm just taking a step away."

She shakes her head. Her disappointment cuts like a knife. "I never thought I'd see the day when you gave up without a fight. Did I make you this way, Finn?"

"Losing you made me a lot of things, angel. But none of that is your fault."

Chapter Twelve

Rissa

A couple of days later, I'm in the office early to get a head start on some paperwork. I'm not a fan of paperwork under any circumstances but my level of cranky this morning has nothing to do with all the tax forms on my screen. It's because I've been sleeping at my mom's house all week instead of at Finn's place.

I hit one of the keys too hard and chip a nail. My frustration is more than just sexual. It's that I'm not on board with this stupid plan of Finn's to take things slowly. His definition of slowly is staying away from me. For the last few days I've only seen him when I'm there to clean. And cleaning the random vacant apartments that he wants move-in ready isn't the same as cleaning his place where I get to see him. Talk to him.

I feel like I'm going through withdrawal and I need a Finn fix.

After ten minutes, I get up and take some aspirin. Staring at a computer screen for hours on end has the tendency to trigger my headaches and I don't have time to be sidelined today. Daphne, Tara and I had a long talk about delegating and trust. Eventually we decided to start the paperwork to bring three of the girls who've been with us the longest into management positions. With three others who can supervise the bigger jobs it will free up some of our time and allow us to have lives again. For the first time in ages, I have a weekday evening free.

My goal is to make it so that none of us work more than ten hours a day. Maybe after a while we can see about cutting it back even more. We might even achieve this mysterious work-life balance that I've heard so much about.

After I've been working for about an hour, I take a break and massage my eyes. I'm going to have to double-check everything I just did since my mind keeps wandering. How can I concentrate on something as mundane as tax regulations when Finn has my mind all twisted? He scares me one minute and then he does something thoughtful the next. How can one man be so sweet and so infuriating at the same time?

The upside to Finn being on his best behavior is that we're talking more and more. What he did for Major Halliwell is part of a bigger program that he's started to help get homeless veterans off the street. It's a nice feeling to be a part of something so important. My crankiness subsides a little as I remember that day. Maybe that's what I need, to focus on the good things. I smile remembering how pleased he looked as he welcomed some of the new tenants. The joy on their faces and his was an honor to witness.

"Whatever you're working on must be way more interesting than anything I've got going on."

I open my eyes to see Tara leaning against the doorframe. Her dark hair is pulled back so only the blue streak is hanging loose.

"Are you aware that you're just staring into space with an incredibly goofy grin on your face?"

I deliberately make my goofy grin even bigger. "Is smiling a crime now?"

"It is when this grin has something to do with a certain moody client of ours."

My smile fades. "I'm trying not to think about him but I can't help it. He's just ... everything that he was when I knew him before and more." I tell her about Major Halliwell. "Instead of cleaning, he's got me helping him out with this new program. It's been a long time since I've felt that good about something I was doing. I really love being a part of that."

Tara's face falls. "You're in love with him. The first day you told me about him, I knew this was where it was going. But it scares me to see how into this guy you are."

"I can't help it, Tara. I've always loved him." It thrills me and frustrates me, too. Wanting Finn is just a constant that I can't escape in my life.

She perches on the edge of my desk. "I know he's gorgeous and rich and crazy over you. But he's also kind of twisted and obsessed and messed up, too. He's already admitted that he wanted to use you and get you out of his system. I just don't want to see you get hurt by this guy. Not again."

"That's just it, I hurt him. He never hurt me. Not once. I was scared when I saw him acting so crazy that day but now that I know what was going on, how can I not try to help him?"

"Gah!" She crosses her arms. "That's our fatal flaw as women. We always want to help guys and nurture them. Sometimes there isn't any help other than to run far and fast."

The nagging pain behind my eye socket has gotten worse and the whole left side of my head is throbbing. I've ignored the signs and now it looks like this is about to develop into a full-blown migraine.

"I need to go home." I wince as another throb of pain stabs right behind my eye. "I'm getting a migraine."

Tara knows how intense my migraines can be so she immediately takes my arm and pulls me to my feet. "Go home and rest. I'll cover for you this afternoon."

"Thank you." I shut down my computer and then walk out to the parking lot. All I really want is to go to Finn's but with the way we left things, I'm not sure if that's such a good idea. Letting him take care of me is really tempting though. He always knew what to do for me when I would get these debilitating headaches.

He always knows what to do in every situation but I'm afraid to get used to relying on that too soon.

* * * * *

The front door has never seemed so far away. The chime peals again and I heave myself upward. I place a hand on my abdomen as I shuffle down the hallway praying that I don't get nauseated again before I can get rid of whoever it is at the door.

I peer through the peephole and then freeze. Finn stands on my mother's front porch looking almost too big for the area the peephole covers. I pull the door open slowly and look at him blearily.

His eyes drift up to my hair and I reach up and pat the haphazard bun that I pulled my curls into. Then I look down at what I'm wearing. I've got on my favorite pair of pajamas with the ribbons and hearts all over them.

Embarrassment sets in. I'm not too exhausted to feel mortified that he's seeing me like this.

"What are you doing here?"

He holds up the plastic bags in his hands. "Delivery." He pushes past me and I just let it happen. I'm way too tired to protest his high-handed methods the way I usually would.

He takes everything to the kitchen and then is back before I can even drag my weary body after him. "I called the office and Tara told me you were sick. How are you feeling?

I push the hair around my face back. "About how I look."

He nods once and then picks me up.

"Finn!"

"You looked like you were on the verge of collapsing at any moment."

"Just tired." Even saying the words requires more energy than I have at the moment.

In my room, he deposits me gently in the middle of the bed. He pulls the covers back so I can slide beneath and then to my surprise, he slides in next to me. It feels so good to have him here. Like I can finally relax and let someone else take care of things for a while.

"Sleep, angel." He loops one arm over my waist and pulls me back into the cradle of his body.

When I wake up the next time, the television is on, the soft lights flickering over the bed. The curtains are drawn so I can't tell whether it's still daylight but I have the sense that it's late. I turn my head and my nose brushes up against Finn's chest. That's when I realize why I'm so warm and cozy. I'm tucked up under Finn's arm, snuggled against his chest.

He stayed with me.

Finn looks down at me and there's something indefinably warm in his expression. This is how he used to look at me, like he could spend hours just staring at my face. "You're awake. Are you hungry?"

My stomach pitches at the idea of food. "No food. I can't even think about it."

He sits up slightly and the motion forces me to move back. "Here. Take a sip of water. You can't get dehydrated."

I sip from the cup he holds out obediently. My migraines always hit me pretty hard and I feel like a wet dishrag that's been wrung out. "Thank you. I feel a little better now. I just needed to sleep."

Now that I don't feel quite so delirious, I can fully appreciate the situation. Finn is snuggled up against me. His chest is bare and I glance down at the bottom half of his body buried beneath the covers. Is he naked under there?

He sees me looking and that shit-eating grin of his is back. "I've got pants on angel, don't get any ideas. I'm sure Gloria would kill me if she thought I was in here debauching you."

"Are you kidding? She'd probably cheer. She's always liked you." I try to sit up and the room sways slightly. I'm bone tired and I'm groggy as if I've been asleep for a very long time.

"Did Daphne come by to clean this morning?" Before I'd left, I'd sent her a text asking her to do it if she had time. Even though this was clearly not a typical job, Finn was still paying for our services. And I really don't want to feel that I'm earning that paycheck on my back.

Finn nods. "She did. That was interesting. First I had to get out of bed to let her in. Then, she accidentally walked in on me while I was dressing because, I assume, you didn't tell her that the master bedroom was off-limits. That was quite a shock for both of us."

I can only imagine. Daphne's probably no longer speaking to me. I definitely should have warned her not to go in his room. I'm also a little jealous that Daphne has seen him half-naked.

"You know you didn't need to send her over. I'm not going to fire you if you skip a date."

"I know that but I've seen how you live. You need daily cleaning."

His soft laughter is a relief. I wasn't sure if he was going to be pissed that I'd done that without asking.

"No, what I need is daily doses of Rissa. But you still look exhausted and that means I haven't been taking care of you properly. So hush and go back to sleep, angel."

There was a time when his proprietary manner would have annoyed me. I'd had more than enough of men thinking they owned me and viewing me as their responsibility. But with Finn I know that he doesn't view taking care of me as an obligation at all. More like an honor. He seems pleased just to be here with me while I'm resting. But I'm reluctant to close my eyes again because I'm afraid this whole thing might turn out to be dream. Then I'll be back to how I was this morning, cranky and depressed because Finn has decided to stay away from me.

I wrap one hand around his neck and pull him down into a kiss. His lips move against mine hungrily and I know that it's been just as hard for him to hold back as it's been for me. Our physical connection is so strong that it's hard to be near him and not be affected. Even now, my body is aching and wet, my pussy clenching hard every time he rocks against me. His mouth is so hot and hard on mine, like he's trying to devour me.

"Damn it, Rissa. You're sick and I still can't keep my hands off you." He pulls back and looks into my eyes. He looks tortured and I can see the strain holding back is having on him.

My other hand trails down his back and then stops on his ass. "I don't want you to keep your hands off me."

"Shit. Your mother is out there."

For some reason that makes me want to giggle. I bury my face against his chest to muffle my soft snickers. "We aren't in high school. This shouldn't be so funny that we're still sneaking around!"

The soft puff of his laughter washes over my cheek. "It's not like I'm climbing up to your bedroom window or something. I'm just trying not to have your mother come in here and hit me with a frying pan."

I stroke him, watching his eyes darken. "We can be quiet."

He groans when I bring my other hand into the mix and grip him through the front of his jeans. "You can't be quiet, angel. And neither can I."

"It would be fun to try though, wouldn't it?" I unbutton the top of his jeans and then carefully lower the zipper.

"Protection. I don't have a condom. I'm clean but—"

"I'm on the pill and I'm clean too. You're running out of excuses, big boy."

Suddenly he grips my hips and tugs on the drawstring bottoms of my pajamas. I lift up and push them down. I wasn't wearing panties underneath anyway.

"You are an unbelievable tease, do you know that?"

I grip him firmly, positioning him right at the center of my core. Right where I need him. "It's not teasing if you follow through."

Then I angle my hips and tug on his ass. The first stroke seats him so deeply that I almost scream right then and there.

"Uh uh, angel. You have to be quiet," he rasps in my ear. The rumble of his deep voice in my ear is sexy as hell.

Then he works himself a little deeper, swiveling his hips slightly as he thrusts. I bite my lip. The pleasure is so intense and every pump of his hips takes me higher. It's incredibly erotic to just lie here while he fucks me, unable to scream or make any noise. The constraint of not being able to make noise makes me more aware of my breathing. My heart rate.

A small whimper escapes when his hands tuck under my bottom, holding me tighter as he thrusts faster. His mouth covers mine and the next sound I make is muffled as he slips his tongue in my mouth. I come just like that feeling completely open and dominated, completely consumed by him.

I can tell his release is close by the way his breath starts coming faster. I wrap my legs around him and clamp down on him every time he withdraws. His fingers on my hips tighten and I'm sure I'll have bruises later. *But it'll be so worth it*, I think as he lets out a harsh groan in my ear. We lie together, panting quietly until he finally moves to the side.

He pulls me back against him again. Part of me wants to just sob at the pleasure of feeling him here, next to me but that would take more energy than I have to expend. For now, it's enough just that he's here.

"I missed you. So much. Don't stay away from me, Finn. I know you think it's best for me but it's not. This is what I need." At another time, when I'm not so sleepy and satisfied, I'll probably regret my candor. But right now I don't care. It's how I feel and I'm tired of pretending.

"I need you, too. And I won't be staying away from you for much longer. There's just something I have to take care of first."

"What do you have to take care of?" I ask but the question is interrupted by a giant yawn.

His lips brush over my forehead. "Right now, you need to sleep. Close your eyes, angel. I'll still be here when you wake up. Then we'll talk."

* * * * *

The next morning I roll over and clutch the pillow I'm holding tighter. I always sleep like the dead after I've had a migraine and last night was no exception. Especially since Finn was there. I always sleep better when he's there.

I open my eyes and frown at the empty space next to me. I prop myself up on my elbow and look around. The house is quiet but the pillow still has the slight indentation where his head rested. Why would Finn sneak out in the middle of the night? Then I catch a glance at the clock on the dresser and scramble to get out of bed. It's almost nine, way later than I usually get in to work. I only hope the other girls haven't needed me for anything.

After a lightning fast shower, I dress in a white T-shirt and jeans, pulling my Maid-4-U logo apron on over it. I pick up my purse and pull out my cell phone. I frown. There are little red flags everywhere. I've never had so many unread texts, voicemails and emails simultaneously before.

I quickly scan the texts. The oldest one is from Finn. He had some meeting this morning and didn't want to wake me. The rest are all from Daphne and Tara. Same with the voicemails. Once I see that my emails are mainly from my partners, too, I call the office with a sinking feeling in my chest.

Daphne answers on the first ring. "Thank god, Rissa. You have to get in to the office."

"What is going on? I have so many messages to listen to."

Daphne pauses. "We just got a call from Mercers. They've been sold and the new owner isn't renewing our contract."

I clap a hand over my mouth. We knew this was a possibility. I'd heard rumors over the years that the owners of Mercers wanted to sell and relocate but they were being really choosy about potential buyers. They wanted to sell to someone with long ties to the community and there aren't many people in this area with that kind of money.

For some reason that thought causes a curl of dread to unfurl in my belly. "Well, this sucks for sure but maybe we can change the owner's mind. They might just be saying that because they want to keep their options open."

Daphne doesn't say anything and the dread in my stomach explodes. "Who is it, Daph? Who's the new owner?"

"Are you coming in? We have a lot of stuff to talk about."

It's a classic Daphne evasion tactic. She hates conflict and she'll

171

do anything to avoid it. Tara and I have been teasing her for years that she could probably teach the military about escape and evade maneuvers. It's usually amusing but then again I'm usually not on the receiving end of it. I take a deep breath so I won't end up yelling at one of my best friends. Then she'll cry and I'll really feel like an ogre.

"You're avoiding the question, Daphne. That doesn't make me feel too good so just spit it out."

"I really think you should come in to the office," she squeaks.

"Daphne!"

She's quiet and then whispers, "I'm sure he has an explanation."

My head is still slightly fuzzy from my extended sleep from the night before. It takes a minute for what she's saying to even register and for me to realize what "he" she's even talking about. When I finally get it, I fall back onto the bed, my legs suddenly unable to hold up my weight anymore.

"Oh god. It's not possible." That's truly how I feel. How could it be possible for Finn to have done something this underhanded? *This manipulative.*

I think back to what he said to me in the elevator earlier this week about not being a good guy. I'd taken it as a sign of self-deprecation but maybe he was trying to warn me. He told me he was an asshole and I didn't listen. I should have heeded the warning.

"I'm so sorry, honey." Daphne's sorrow comes over the line and blends with mine. She hates giving bad news and this is probably even worse for her since she knows how I feel about Finn.

"This just can't be real. Are you sure?"

"Tara said the new company's name is the same one on our paperwork when we did the deal with Finn. Unless this is all a really big coincidence."

"Or he's been playing me this whole time."

Chapter Thirteen

Rissa

Daphne, Tara and I have closeted ourselves in my office. I've looked at the contract we signed a dozen times, hoping that the letters on the page will rearrange somehow and form something else. But there's no denying that the name matches the new owner of Mercers.

The previous owners were super helpful when I called back and very apologetic about everything. I'm sure they know how important their contract is to our business so I could tell they felt bad about the effect this will have on us. But it's not their fault that I trusted the wrong man.

That's no one's fault but my own.

"Maybe it isn't what it looks like?" Daphne suggests. She's been hovering over me ever since I got here. I think she feels some sense of responsibility since she had to break the news to me. But it doesn't matter who told me or how I found out. All that matters is the bottom line.

Finn Marshall now owns me in truth.

"Or maybe it's exactly what it looks like." My head falls forward into my hands. Not only am I humiliated because I've been so stupid and so blind but also completely sick that I have let my two best friends down. They've done nothing but support me and now because of Finn's vendetta against me, they are going to be caught up in the crossfire.

"He warned me. He told me in the very beginning that he wanted revenge and that was his sole purpose in seeking me out."

"He actually said that?" Daphne asks, horrified.

Tara squeezes her arm. "Let's not get ahead of ourselves. There may be another explanation. Maybe he was already in the process of buying Mercers before you guys reconnected?"

It's possible but in my heart I know it isn't true. My mom always told me not to trust pretty words from a man. To just take them at face value and I've never been good at that. If I had heeded that advice, then I would have run away the first time I saw Finn standing in the middle of his apartment looking so haunted.

"He would have told me about it if that were the case. It came up in conversation way too many times. No, this was deliberate. I know it was."

Finally Tara speaks what we're all thinking. "But if he's doing this for revenge, then that means we just lost two major contracts. And we can't meet payroll without at least one of them."

I nod, miserable. If I hadn't already done the paperwork to push a couple of our part-timers into full-time status it wouldn't be so bad. But we now have more salaries along with the resultant benefits and taxes to pay. Along with our next rent payment, we're screwed.

Totally and completely screwed.

"How could he even know that was one of our major clients in time to pull this off?" Tara wonders.

"Oh god." The humiliations just keep on coming. I bang my forehead against the desk. "The presentation. When his lawyer asked for the quote, he also asked for references. You know, other clients so they can check up on you. That presentation gave him everything he needed to figure out our weak spots. I wouldn't be surprised if he didn't try to buy all of our other clients. That's how he does things. All or nothing."

"This is pretty sick. There has to be something we can do." Tara paces the floor and then blows out a breath. "Maybe we should go and talk to him. All three of us. We can threaten to sue or go to the media! How would he like that? I'm sure the local news would cover that story. *Billionaire asshole bankrupts three local women for funzies*."

I snort out a laugh. Even in the midst of a crisis Tara can always make me laugh. Then my smile fades. "I'll go talk to him. He's mad at me so it follows that I'm the one he wants to hurt the most. Maybe if I tell him what he's really done, he'll stop this. There's plenty of other ways he can hurt just me without taking away the employment of a bunch of women who need their jobs."

"Do you really think that'll work?" Daphne looks hopeful. I don't want to crush her optimism but I'm afraid to give her anything to hold on to.

"No, I really don't think that'll work. But I'm hoping that underneath the part of him that obviously still hates me, that there's still a piece of the boy I loved. That guy was always a good person." I stand up and grab my handbag.

"Let's just hope he's still in there somewhere."

* * * * *

Even though I have a key, I ring the bell. Finn opens the door after a few minutes.

"Rissa? What are you doing out here? Did you lose your key?"

He opens the door wider and steps back so I can enter. After a moment of hesitation, I come in. With the exception of that day when he was hallucinating, he's never scared me. I'm just afraid of what he makes me feel.

"I already know Finn, so you can drop the act. Your plan succeeded. Congratulations."

He looks so thoroughly confused that for a moment a small ray of hope peeks through that maybe this is all a mistake.

"What plan?"

"Your revenge. Your plan to buy all my clients so that I'll be wholly and completely dependent on you."

Suddenly he looks wary. "What are you talking about?"

"Mercers. They were just bought out. By your company."

He looks shocked and then I see it. Recognition. He knew this was happening.

His eyes close briefly. "Rissa wait. I can explain."

Those words should be banned from the male vocabulary because that's the first thing men say when they've done something wrong. Andy always had an explanation too after he'd hurt me and I'm done with listening to people rationalizing away my pain.

"There's nothing that needs explanation. I'm stupid for trusting. You were honest from the very beginning. You told me that this was your way of working me out of your system and that you wanted to hurt me the way I hurt you. Well, I just thought you should know that your plan worked brilliantly."

I can feel the tears coming but I refuse to cry in front of him. That's what he wants. He wanted to break me down. To make me pay. It hurts so much to think back over the last few weeks, to find out that all those moments that I thought we were reconnecting were really just part of some grand master plan to ruin me. I've had more fun with him than I've had with anyone. Ever. How can I trust anybody again if this isn't real? How can I trust anything I feel?

"Rissa, listen to me. In the beginning I did want to hurt you. I told my lawyer to keep his eyes open for the opportunity to buy any of the companies listed as your clients. I admit that."

I gape at him. "You say that like it's not a big deal. Like it's not the worst violation ever."

"That's not what I meant. I know that it was wrong. And as soon as we started talking again, things started to change. All the ways I wanted to hurt you, I wanted to help you. Being around you reminded me of how I used to be. Carefree. Happy."

"Well, being around you has reminded me that I'm just as naive as ever. Because once again I've let myself get involved with someone who has an ulterior motive. Someone who wants to control me."

"I don't want to control you. My plan was to buy out all your clients just so you'd see me. I wanted you to know that I could crush you. The way you crushed me all those years ago. But I gave it up just as soon as I got to know you again. I told my lawyer to stop looking for deals. I didn't realize that he'd already finalized this one. He has power of attorney to complete deals for this company without my signature. I didn't even know he'd done it until today. I thought that I had time to fix it. I was going to tell you."

I laugh so hard it actually hurts my stomach. Finn just stands watching me like he's afraid to come any closer. Which shows he really is a smart one because if he gets too close right now I might just scratch his eyes out.

"That's your defense? You've been accused of lying, manipulating and just being downright diabolical and your defense is *my lawyer did it*?"

Finn sighs. "I was going to tell you. I just thought I had more time to figure things out. I'll fix this and then things can go back to the way they were."

How could I not have seen this in him before now, that he will spin, cajole and manipulate any situation regardless of how wrong it may be? Has he really been like this all along and I just couldn't see it? Or did I do this to him?

Maybe this is my penance for my past sins. To reconnect with the man I love only to find that he's been destroyed and twisted by what I did to him.

"All that time you were telling me you loved me and all the while you were scheming behind my back to bankrupt my business. But it's not just my business, Finn. It's Tara's and Daphne's and the women who work for us. They're all hurt too and it isn't fair because they have nothing to do with our history."

I hold up my hand when he moves closer. All the things that he'll say to convince me are probably already poised on his lips for a perfect delivery. Finn has always been a master at that and I'm sure with enough time he could wear me down and convince me that I'm overreacting. But I don't want to let him sway me this time.

"Things can't go back to the way they were."

I sit down on the arm of the couch, suddenly exhausted and depressed. The second wind I'd gotten when I found out about his treachery is deserting me now leaving me with the same lingering lethargy I had when I first woke up.

Briefly, I wish that I could rewind and go back to this morning. I would roll over, put the pillow over my head and ignore the world. We never truly enjoy our last moments of calm.

"Please just let me try to fix this, Rissa. I'll sell the company to someone else with the contingency that they have to use your company's services. Or I'll keep it and then you'll know for sure that you have the contract as long as you want it."

He sounds so sincere, one shade close to begging and for a moment, I almost give in. But where does it end if I do that? Will he buy all my other clients? Will he buy the grocery store where I shop or the salon where I get my hair done? Where will his sphere of control end? It'll be just like before when I lived with Andrew, scared to tell anyone how he treated me because I was wholly dependent on him for survival.

Never again.

"No matter what spin you try to put on this, it comes down to the same thing. You want to control me just like Andrew did. And I'm over that."

* * * * *

Driving home, I have to pull over three times because I'm crying so hard. I don't want to have an accident or endanger anyone else but I really just want to get home. I need my bed and my mom and to block out everything to do with manipulative men.

But then again I really don't want my mom to see me like this. So I decide instead to return to my house. *Andrew's house,* I correct myself. I have to stop thinking of it as my home. It never really was.

I pull up in the driveway and my eyes are immediately drawn to the white sign taped to the door. I get out, not bothering to lock up my car, and march across the lawn. My neighbor on the left side is outside weeding. When she sees me on the warpath toward the front door, she jumps up and runs inside her house.

That's right. Go call and tell him I'm here.

I snatch the paper off the door and scan the document quickly. It's some kind of notice that says I have three days to vacate the property for failure to pay rent.

That bastard.

Andrew is pissed so this is how he decides to punish me. By throwing me out with very little warning. It shouldn't even come as a surprise to me since this is exactly the kind of thing he does. Underhanded. Juvenile. Manipulative.

My taste in men is consistent at least.

I pull out my phone. "Tara. I'm so sorry to do this but can you come to my house? Andy has put some kind of eviction notice on the door and I'll need help getting my stuff out."

She promises to bring Daphne with her before she hangs up. Briefly, I realize that even though promoting three people is probably what's going to bankrupt us, at least it means that the girls and I have more time to deal with all this crap.

I ball up the paper and open the door with my key. It smells slightly musty after being closed up for the past few weeks. I flip the deadbolt and then go upstairs to the master bedroom. The majority of the furniture was stuff that Andrew bought for us so I don't want any of that. I throw most of my clothes in my suitcase and then zip it closed. I already packed most of my essentials when I moved into my mom's house so the only things left are my out of season clothes and some of my books.

I pack my favorite paperbacks into a duffel bag and then wrestle both the duffel and the suitcase down the stairs. I hear a car in the driveway and look out the window. Andy steps out of his white SUV. When he sees me in the window, he waves with a little smirk on his face.

I rush over to the front door and pull it open. I quickly flip the lock on the glass storm door and then close the front door again. He has a key to the main door but I'm willing to bet he doesn't have one for the storm door. I'm not even sure if I have it.

A muffled curse from the other side of the door proves me right. "Rissa! Open the damn door."

"Go away Andrew or I'm calling the police!"

"You can't lock me out, this is my house!"

I hear him fumbling with the latch again and then I hear a muffled thud.

"Son of a bitch!"

I look out of the peephole but I can't see anything. Then I hear Tara's voice.

"Hello, 911. Yes, Andrew Carrington is harassing my friend at her home. Yes, right now. You know I'm not sure if he's armed or not. It's probably better to assume he is. Maybe you should send a SWAT team and tell the local news to come too."

I run to the window just in time to see Andy jump behind the wheel of his SUV and reverse out of the driveway. Tara runs behind him and then throws something at the back of the car. It connects with the back bumper and Andrew swerves slightly.

Good one, Tara.

I run back to the front door and pull it open. Daphne looks terrified and launches herself into my arms. "Rissa! Are you okay?"

"I'm fine, thanks to you guys. I'm so glad you're here." I hug her back, then start laughing when I see the muddy rock on the front step.

"Did you throw that at him?" I ask Tara when she approaches.

She sniffs. "Damn right I did. And I'm bummed that my aim is so bad. I thought for sure I'd nail him in the face with that one."

"Did you actually call the cops?" Daphne looks impressed.

Tara makes a face. "No, I actually didn't have time to dial anything. I just wanted to scare him off. He's such an asshole." She looks down at her phone and then hits a few keys.

"Who are you calling now?" Daphne asks.

"No one." Tara pockets her phone but she won't meet my eyes.

She looks behind me to the suitcase and duffel I dropped in the middle of the entryway. "Come on let's box up your stuff and get it over to your Mom's house before that jerk comes back. I don't feel like going to jail today."

Chapter Fourteen

Finn

As evening descends, I sit staring at my phone. I've been on calls all morning, trying to figure out what I should do.

How could I have screwed this up so badly?

Patrick Stevens had several suggestions and I've considered everything from selling the company to outright gifting it to Marissa.

But in the end, I know it actually won't make any difference. Even if I could convince the Mercers to buy it back, the damage is already done. Rissa has seen just how far I'll go when I want something and how ruthless I can be when I consider someone an enemy.

It wasn't about the company it was about the reason why I'd purchased it in the first place.

My plan didn't seem to have any downsides in the beginning. My image of Rissa was of a beautiful materialistic liar, a girl who left me when I needed her the most. But after just a few days with her, I knew even then that I was wrong.

Worse, I wasn't the only one who'd felt betrayed. The things that I'd done and said had contributed to our relationship falling apart just as much as her decision to choose someone else. Maybe if I hadn't been deployed part of the time I could have seen the cracks in our relationship before it was too late. But I was so caught up in my jealousy and anger that all I could see was that she'd left me. And I'd felt completely justified in devising my plan to punish her.

I would have never thought we'd end up as friends again and definitely not lovers.

All at once, I become aware of the time. I've been sitting in this room all day. I've missed my usual visit with my mother. If I leave now, I can get over there before it gets too late. She goes to bed earlier now and sleeps longer.

I pull out my phone to call Jonah and then put it away. I grab the keys I keep on the kitchen counter and ride the elevator down to the parking level. Then I climb up into the old Ford pickup that I've had for ages.

When I get to my mom's house, Tank's motorcycle is in the drive and lights are on all over the house. Part of me wants to turn around and go back home but I park in the drive next to my brother's bike and get out. It's time I stopped hiding from the people who love me and let them help me.

I open the door with my key. Emma looks up from the couch. "Finn! You actually came this time?"

My face must show that I have no idea what she's talking about because she gets up. "Tank told me he's invited you to dinner with us a few times but you're always too busy."

Her eyes are kind and I could easily take the out that she's given me. But I'm tired of allowing other people to make excuses for my bad behavior.

"My brother was trying to keep me from looking like a selfish jerk. I'm not too busy, I've just been too wrapped up in my own shit to care about being a real part of this family. I'm sorry for that. I'm going to try to do better."

Emma looks stunned but recovers quickly. "I'm really glad to hear that. Why don't we go into the kitchen? I'm sure Claire is going to be really happy to see you."

I walk beside her and then it occurs to me how odd it is for her not to be in the kitchen anyway. "What are you doing out here? Did Mom banish you from the kitchen again?"

She looks at me from the corner of her eye. "Maybe."

"So, you're using me as an excuse to get back in there?"

"Hey, don't judge me."

We're still laughing when we enter the kitchen. Mom is at the stove stirring something. She looks up and when she sees Emma, she frowns. "You're supposed to be reading a magazine!"

Emma holds up her hands. "I'm not interfering, I promise. I was just coming in to tell you that Finn is here. That's all."

Mom narrows her eyes at Emma playfully. "I know you're dying to get in here and take over."

Emma pouts. "It's your dinner. I promised I wouldn't interfere and I won't."

Mom shakes her head. "Go ahead. I know it's killing you."

We watch as Emma runs over to the pot and tastes whatever's on the spoon. She reaches for some kind of spice on the counter and shakes a little in.

I look over at Mom. "Well, that made her happy."

"You've made me happy. I'm glad to see you here. But you don't look right. What's happened?" Suddenly she looks behind me expectantly. "Did you bring Marissa with you?"

I shake my head and she seems to instantly know. She turns to Emma who is still happily puttering behind the stove. "Emma, sweetheart would you mind keeping an eye on things? I'm going to sit down."

Then she pulls me into the living room and pushes me toward the sofa with more strength than I would have expected.

"Finn Marshall, you tell me what you did!"

I've never been good at explaining myself and this situation is strangely reminiscent of when I used to get in trouble as a kid.

"I hurt her."

The whole story comes spilling out and to her credit, Mom doesn't interrupt me. I go through the whole thing from my plan to rub Rissa's face in my newfound wealth, to our run ins with her ex, to falling in love with her and even the night I was higher than a kite and scared her to death. Mom listens to it all, sitting quietly on the couch next to me, her hands folded neatly in her lap.

I've just finished telling her about how Rissa found out about it all when she finally speaks.

"I always thought something was wrong between Andrew and Rissa. After you guys broke up and you deployed again, she never really looked happy. But I'm really surprised by this Finn. I raised you better than this."

I hang my head, knowing that her shame in my behavior is completely warranted.

"You've hurt a really lovely young woman and all because of pride. I'm sure that you want to get her back but I don't think you're in a place to even think about that yet."

I glance over at her. "But I have to make her see. She'll hate me if I can't find a way to explain this."

"Love is a powerful thing and I think that if you give her some time and show her through your actions that you've changed, that she might be able to forgive you. But the most important thing is that you're not healthy. And you haven't addressed that." She pulls me into a hug. "I blame myself for some of this. I knew that something wasn't right. All those pills disappearing. I think in my heart, I knew and I just didn't want to see it."

"It's not your fault, Mom. I only took the unfinished bottles when you got a new prescription. There's no way you could have known that. You've got more than enough on your own plate worrying about your own health."

She pins me with a hard look. "I'm a mother. Our plates expand. There's never so much going on that I don't worry about my children. That will never change."

I think about all the things she's gone through in her life. She was abandoned by my father, worked all sorts of jobs including a stint as a stripper to support us. Through it all, my mother has never lost her dignity. Because she was doing it all to protect her family. The only person I've been protecting all this time is myself.

"I looked up rehab centers. There's a private clinic in West Haven that can admit me next week. I have to get help. I was planning to do that even before Rissa found out about this."

Saying it out loud is a little scary but it also strengthens my resolve. I want to be the kind of person that my family, that Rissa can be proud of. I want to look in the mirror and be proud of myself. Going into rehab is the only way I can make that happen.

She nods and then puts her hand on my shoulder. "We'll be there for you, you know that. No matter what. But nothing else you do will matter if you don't get yourself healthy first."

Tank appears in the doorway. "Hey, man. When did you get here?" The strange hairless cat he adopted when he first started dating Emma winds around his legs and then disappears behind the recliner in the corner.

"Poochie, come out." Tank snaps his fingers. "We're trying to get her to be more social."

Mom gives me a look. Despite how dark I'm feeling, it brings a smile to my face. The only person Tank's cat likes is Tank. And maybe Emma. It definitely hates me.

"Dinner's ready!" Emma calls out.

My mom pats my leg and then stands. "I'll help set the table. You boys wash up and come on."

My phone rings. I look down to see I have a text from an unfamiliar number.

I'm still mad at you but I just thought you should know. Andrew was at the house messing with Rissa earlier. - - Tara

Tank gives up on coaxing the cat out and then glances over at me. "Are you staying? Or do you have to leave?"

I look up. "I'm staying. I just need to make a phone call."

"Good. I'm glad you made time." He walks into the kitchen. As soon as he's gone, the cat comes out from behind the recliner and hisses at me. "Okay, okay. I'm going." I walk into the other room to make my call.

Jonah answers on the first ring.

"First I want to apologize because this is absolutely not in your job description. However, I need you to keep an eye on Miss Blake tonight. Follow discreetly and do not engage. But I need to know that she's safe."

"Of course, sir. I'll let you know if anything doesn't look right."

"Thank you."

I hang up and move back into the living room. For a moment, I just stand there listening to the comforting sounds of family. When I close my eyes, I can picture the scene: Mom moving around getting plates and silverware, Emma at the stove, Tank behind her trying to sneak kisses in when no one is looking.

This is how I want to remember them while I'm gone. The memory will hold me over while I do the hard work of getting my life back on track. Maybe by then I'll finally be in a place where I feel I deserve to convince Rissa to give me another chance.

* * * * *

Dinner was the usual loud, happy affair. Mom didn't make any mention of our earlier conversation and I was more than happy to let Tank and Emma carry the conversation. Halfway through dinner, we found out why Emma was so happy that I'd come when she pulled her hand from her pocket wearing a massive engagement ring.

The rest of the evening was champagne toasts and wedding planning. Emma wants to get married in the spring so they have less than a year to plan everything. Mom and Emma started talking about dresses and cake tasting and Tank looked like his eyes were glazing over by the end of it. I'm pretty sure my brother has no idea what he's in for over the next few months.

I pull into my parking space and check my phone again. Jonah hasn't reported anything so I have to assume that means Rissa is fine. I'm going to have to adjust to not knowing where she is all the time or if she's safe. I haven't earned the right to that yet. Thinking about that just fuels my determination to get started cleaning up my life.

Once I'm upstairs, I open my cabinets and grab all the pill bottles. I carry them over to the living room table and dump them in a big pile. Then I walk back to the bathroom and open the medicine chest in there. I pull out more bottles, some of them with my name on them, some of them in my mom's name, and carry them up front too.

I sit down on the couch and stare at the pile, forcing myself to see what I've become. I have a stash. A fucking stash that I've amassed by lying to my mother. Then the insidious voice of doubt creeps in.

Isn't it a bad thing to kick medication cold turkey?

Maybe I should keep taking them until I get checked in somewhere.

I've been doing it this long so what will one more hurt?

My head hurts from all the thoughts rolling around in my head. From the decisions I need to make. Before I know what's happened one of the pill bottles is in my hand. I shake out a few. Then I shake out a few more. I close my hand around the pills and squeeze.

I hear the door open behind me but I don't bother to turn around. When Tank sits next to me on the couch, he doesn't say anything. I knew he'd find his way here eventually.

"What happened?"

"Mom didn't tell you?"

"I asked her not to. I figured it might be something that you wanted to keep private. I'm asking you directly so you can decide if you want to tell me or not."

That surprises me. My mom hasn't been particularly good at keeping secrets in the past. But I know this is Tank's way of supporting me. And I know he'll be here to help me however I need him to, whether I tell him what happened or not.

"Short version, I fucked it up."

He nods. "Okay, so how are you going to fix it?"

One of the best things about Tank is that he likes to get right to the point. He doesn't really need a lot of details just goes right to solutions. I also know that if I need him to, he'll sit here with me all night patiently waiting until I'm ready to confide in him. Silence doesn't bother him at all. He uses the time to watch and collect information that might prove useful. It's what made him such a great sniper.

"I'm going to ask for help." Before I can change my mind or doubts can make me second-guess myself, I extend my hand toward him and uncurl my fingers. The mess of pills sits in my palm, sweaty from being squeezed in my hand for so long. "Don't let me fuck up anything else, Tank."

He stares at my outstretched hand and then his big hand covers mine, pulling the pills from my grasp. He stands and then disappears from view.

"Are you flushing them?"

He comes back with a plastic trash bag. "I can't do that. Emma has lectured me too many times about how you aren't supposed to flush certain things because it'll get into the water table."

"You are so whipped."

"Hell yeah, I am." He takes his hand and sweeps all the pill bottles on the table into the bag and then ties it closed. "I'm not going to dispose of all these bottles yet. Just in case your doctor wants you to wean off of them. But I'll keep them with me. I'll come over and give them to you when you need them."

"Okay." My eyes follow the bag until he stuffs it into the corner of the couch behind him and out of sight.

When he speaks again, his voice is just as shaky as mine. "All this time, I thought it was Mom. Her pills disappeared so fast and all she would say was that she was misplacing them."

He looks up at me and his eyes are suspiciously bright. It takes a lot to bring out emotion in my big brother but I can see that he's fighting for control. Shame washes over me again.

"I'm sorry. I've let all of you down. And I let you think that our mother was abusing her pills rather than tell you the truth."

His eyes remain on mine as he claps a hand on my shoulder. "It's going to be okay. I promise." He pulls me in for a hug and for a moment, I just allow him to prop me up.

Because I haven't been doing such a great job at that on my own.

After I feel calm enough to speak without crying like a baby, I pull back. "I booked a stay at a private clinic already. Can you drive me over there?"

"Done. Anything you need, you know I've got your back."

"Anything? Because there's someone who has been bothering Rissa lately. I might want us to take a little detour before you drop me off."

His eyes gleam in the semi-darkness. Then he smiles.

Chapter Fifteen

Rissa

Daphne bursts into my office. "Did you hear? It's all over the news!"

I look up from my computer. "No, what's going on?"

"TMZ is reporting that Andrew Carrington was attacked over the weekend. Apparently some random thugs beat him up and then stuffed him in a dumpster. But he refuses to identify who did it to the police."

I turn back to my laptop and then pull up a search engine. A few seconds later I have the gossip site up on my screen. I gasp at the pictures of Andy's bruised and bloody face.

"Oh my god."

Tara enters and puts a stack of folders on the edge of my desk. She leans over my shoulder and then averts her eyes. "Hmm. Are you guys ready to go over the bills again?"

I recognize her guilty face. "Tara, do you know anything about this?"

"Why would I know anything about it? Guys who are assholes get beat up sometimes. It's called karma."

Daphne looks as unconvinced as I feel but I decide to let it go. We have work to do. The weekends have always been our time to go over bills and strategize but with everything going on, we've been putting it off. Usually we try to make it fun by ordering pizza but I don't think any of us are in a fun mood today. I pull up our financial software and we all look at the dangerously low bank balance displayed on the screen.

"I can't believe he actually did it," Daphne whispers. "Even after everything, I didn't think he'd actually back out of paying us. What are we going to do?"

Tara recovers first. "We're going to have to pay the girls and I can take a cut this week."

I turn to her. "No, Tara that's not fair. You need your paycheck just as much as anyone else."

"I have some savings," she insists.

I groan, completely disgusted with myself. Despite all evidence to the contrary, I let my personal feelings for Finn intrude and influence the way I did business. The initial deposit that he paid when we signed the contract will help some but it's not nearly enough to cover the overtime shifts we need to pay out to all the girls who worked so tirelessly to get the second floor of his building ready to occupy in less than two weeks. As angry as I was at him, I should have made sure that we were paid before I confronted him. My impulsive decision might have just cost us our business. We were already on shaky ground and we can't afford to eat this kind of loss.

"It's my fault, so I will be the one who doesn't take a paycheck."

Daphne looks so sad, that I put my arm around her shoulders. She's the most optimistic of us all so stuff like this really takes her by surprise.

"It's okay, Daph. We're going to figure this out. It just means we'll have to cut some of the girls' hours. I don't want to do that but it looks like we don't have a choice."

"I know. It's just that I saw the way he looked at you. I really thought he'd fix it in the end."

We're still sitting in depressed silence when the front door buzzer sounds. Tara hops up. "I'll get it. It's probably just a delivery of supplies."

She returns a few minutes later with a slim envelope. "It's for you, Rissa. It was hand delivered and there's no return address."

I take the envelope. It's not even sealed properly, just fastened with those small metal hooks. I pry them open and then pull out the piece of paper inside. It's a photocopy.

The girls gather around me as I stare in disbelief at the document in my hands. Tara takes the paper from my hands and scrutinizes it. Even once it's out of my hands, I still see the letters in front of my face. It's a certified copy from the county of the deed to a building. To our building.

In my name.

"He did it!" Daphne throws her arms around me. Her enthusiasm is so infectious that I allow her to dance me around in a circle as Tara breaks out into nervous giggles.

"You own the building now." She turns to me. "He actually came through."

"This is so exciting! I knew he would come through. You have to go see him. Right now!" Daphne shoves me down into the desk chair and pulls a brush from her purse.

"My hair is too curly for that. If you brush it, it'll poof up until I look like a poodle."

"Oh right." She throws the brush on the desk and gently finger combs the snarls from my hair. Tara rummages through my purse until she finds my lip-gloss. She hands it to me. I apply a thin layer with shaky hands.

"What am I going to say to him?"

Tara shakes her head. "The man just gave you a building. I'd say all the rules have officially been thrown out the window. I'm pretty sure he won't care what you say. He'll just be glad you're back."

Warmth suffuses me as they rush me out the door. I turn at the last minute. "What if this isn't his way of saying he wants me back? Maybe he's just trying to keep us from suing him."

The idea of going over there by myself only to find out that Finn is still angry terrifies me.

"Come on, we'll drive you. You're not in any shape to drive. Plus, I love to see a happy ending!" Daphne herds me outside and then turns to lock the front doors of the building behind us.

"How do you know it's going to be a happy ending?" I am desperate to know the answer. Because I want that so much and anytime I've ever wanted something like this, it hasn't happened.

"This is your romantic moment, Ris. It's just like in the movies. The hero does something stupid but then he apologizes and does the grand gesture. Then he picks her up and carries her off into the sunset. This is your time to ride off into the sunset and no one deserves it more than you."

Tara leads us to her car since it's the biggest and I climb into the back while Daphne gets up front. They whisper softly back and forth to each other the entire drive but I'm not paying attention to any of it. All I'm thinking of is Finn and what I'll say to him.

Tara parks directly in front of his building. John waves as we enter the lobby. I use my key and then hit the button for the top floor. Tara bumps my shoulder. "Are you ready for this?"

"I hope so."

When we get to his floor, we turn left and then stop in front of his door. I raise my hand to knock and then hesitate. Daphne sighs and then raps on the door with her fist.

I glare at her. "I needed a moment."

"You need to hurry up. Happily ever after waits for no one."

After a minute, we all look at each other before Daphne bangs on the door again. I put my ear on the door listening. Nothing.

I pull out my key ring. Using it is a risk because there's a chance that he's here and just ignoring the door. If I open it, he could be pissed. Or he could be naked with someone else. Any number of humiliating and painful scenarios run through my mind.

But at least then I'd know for sure.

I slide my key in and turn the lock. I push the door open and stick my head around the doorjamb.

"Oh no."

I push the door open all the way and then walk into the apartment. The now completely empty apartment.

Daphne puts her hand over her mouth. "Oh, Rissa. I'm so sorry."

* * * * *

I've been sitting on the floor in the middle of Finn's empty apartment for the last ten minutes. Daphne and Tara are waiting downstairs in the car. I told them I just needed a minute to process. I need more like a lifetime to process this.

"Rissa? What are you doing here?"

I look up. Tank is standing in the doorway holding a roll of duct tape and an empty cardboard box. I hastily wipe away my tears. It's humiliating enough that Finn has just moved on without even saying goodbye to me but I definitely don't want him to find out that I was sitting in the middle of his apartment crying like some kind of stalker chick.

"Nothing. I just came to see Finn but I guess he doesn't want to see me." I look around and laugh weakly.

Tank drops the box on the counter. "I know for a fact that he wants to see you. But he can't."

I watch as he assembles the box and then rolls duct tape over the seams. He's obviously been busy in here to have cleaned out this place so fast.

"Well, tell him I got the deed he sent me. And that I wish him well, wherever he ends up."

Tank looks over at me. "He's going to end up right back here. Would you hand me that roll of bubble wrap over there."

Puzzled by his strange nonchalance, I back up until I see the bubble wrap in the corner of the room. It's right below where the television used to be. There's a faded spot on the wall where the paint is a slightly lighter color.

"What do you mean he's going to end up right back here? Didn't he move out?"

"Nope. He's just getting the place painted. He asked me to move all his stuff out so the painters can come in this week."

Relief buckles my knees and I sit back down on the floor. "What? You mean he's not gone? Is he staying somewhere else? Can you take me to him?"

Suddenly Tank looks uncomfortable. "Um, he is staying somewhere else but I can't take you to him."

It feels like we're talking in circles. Tank was always straight with me so I don't understand why he's being deliberately difficult right now.

"If he doesn't want to see me, just tell me. I don't think I can take any more games." I look around at the mostly empty room. There are so many memories here. But all the good ones are tarnished by that final awful argument. He was trying to apologize even then but I wasn't ready to hear it then. And now that I am, he's gone.

"You're really not going to tell me where he is?"

He puts down the tape. "He's in rehab. And I really don't think he wants you to see him like that. I'm sorry that I'm being so cagey about this but he's my little brother. I just want him to get better."

"I want him to get better, too. There's nothing I want more than that. I would never get in the way of his recovery. I just want to help him."

Things are quiet for a moment and when I look up, Tank is standing next to me. He lowers himself onto the floor next to me. "Damn, I'm too big to be getting down on the floor. I hope you know I wouldn't do this for just anybody."

His cranky commentary brings a brief smile to my face. I know he's trying to make me feel better.

"You know I've always liked you, Rissa. But this situation ... it's just not a good place for my brother. Finn is going to kick my ass when he finds out I said this to you but I think that having you in his life right now might be doing him more harm than good."

"But I love him."

"I know. He loves you, too. The two of you have always been like fireworks. You spark off each other and you create all this heat.

But while fireworks are exciting, they can also be dangerous. And I think he needs a chance to recover before he tackles all the issues you guys have."

Despite the fact that what he's saying mirrors what I've been thinking too, it still hurts to hear. Love is supposed to be enough. No one wants to think of their love as being a force that might hold someone else back.

"So you're saying I have to let him go." I swallow over the lump in my throat. Everything inside me wants to reject what he's saying but I know that he's right.

"Yeah. You have to let him go. Just for a little while."

Chapter Sixteen

Finn

I pull on a pair of comfortable jeans, and then pull out a striped collared shirt. Being in my own place with my own stuff feels weird after being away for the past few weeks. My eyes land on the row of tailored suits in the back of my closet. I had them all made when I got the first part of my inheritance. Flush with more money than sense, I'd wanted to dress a certain way. Like looking the part would make me feel like I deserved the money.

That's always been my way when I'm trying to impress someone. Put on the flash. But today I just want my favorite pair of jeans. I want to look like myself.

Today I'm going to see my girl.

Jonah is waiting for me downstairs. I called him as soon as Tank brought me back from the rehab center. He's been on vacation for the past month visiting his mother in Arizona. He has a deep tan and looks more relaxed than I've ever seen him. When he sees me, he actually smiles.

"It's good to have you back, sir."

"It's great to be back."

He opens the door and I slip into the backseat. Taking my truck out for a spin was my first choice but then I realized I might want my hands free on the ride home.

After I give Jonah the address of our destination, I sit back and think about what I'm going to say.

When I first checked myself into the rehab center, I thought the only way I could handle leaving was to cut off all communication with the outside world completely. But at the last minute, I sent Rissa an email expressing my sincere apologies for my deception. It was important for me to tell her that I was truly sorry for what I'd done. No excuses. No bullshit.

I wasn't even sure if she'd accept my apology but then she'd answered back to tell me she appreciated my gift of the building. I'm not even sure how it happened but over the past six weeks we've exchanged dozens of emails and talked about everything in a way that we had difficulty doing face-to-face.

I told her about my group therapy sessions. She told me about the changes she's made at work to make sure they all have more leisure time. When I was shaking and shivering craving the pills so badly that I wanted to scream, I would read her emails over and over and it gave me something to focus on.

Jonah stops the car at the curb in front of Gloria Blake's house. I know Rissa is still staying here because I had Jonah check before I got back. I could have just asked her but I didn't want to tip my hand. I want to surprise her. According to Jonah, she always leaves for her second shift about this time. She doesn't know this but Tara will be covering for her tonight.

After about ten minutes, Rissa steps outside. She's carrying a bunch of stuff just like usual and when I see her my heart clenches. She locks the door behind her and then looks up to the sky. Her eyes are closed.

I get out of the car and walk up the driveway. She opens her eyes and gapes at me. "Finn?"

"What are you doing out here? It's a little early for stargazing, isn't it?"

Her soft smile is so warm that I can feel it from where I stand. "Just making a wish."

"What did you wish for?"

"It already happened." Then she steps down and leans against my chest.

I pull her into my arms and bury my face in her hair.

"Tank told me that he saw you. He said that he told you where I was but he asked you to stay away." I'd been pretty angry with him that day but that didn't last long. I know that my brother is only trying to look out for me. I would have done the same thing if our positions were reversed for sure.

"He did. I was hurt at first but after I thought about it, I understood. Getting clean had to be about you. Not about us." She lifts her head and wraps both arms around my waist. "I'm so glad you're back. I missed you."

"I missed you, too. You have no idea."

"Are you okay?"

"No."

"Are you in pain?" she whispers.

"Every day."

She looks down at my leg. I made the choice to walk unassisted today. One of the most important parts of detoxing was focusing on the physical symptoms that my addiction was masking. I've been working with a physical therapist. That's something that I should have been doing all along but it was just easier to take the pills and forget the pain.

I can't pretend that it's been easy. Several times over the last six weeks, I've wondered why I ever thought that I could survive unmedicated. But now that I've seen how much I've been missing out on, how much life has been passing me by, I know I'll never go back. My leg still hurts but I've been embracing the pain. It keeps me grounded. It makes me focus. It reminds me that I'm alive.

And it reminds me how lucky I am to be here.

Rissa clenches her hands into fists as if she's trying not to reach out and grab me again. "You should be using your cane."

"I wasn't talking about my leg."

Her eyes meet mine. "I didn't think you were coming back. I really thought that maybe this was just some kind of sign that we're not good for each other and that we're better off apart."

"After everything, all the surgeries and the pain, I struggled for months to come to terms with what I lost. But what I really lost wasn't physical. It was you. And nothing I've done since has ever healed the wound. You are the phantom pain that I cannot escape."

"And you are the piece of my heart that I lost and then found again. What a pair we make." A tear escapes and rolls down her cheek. She swipes it away. "We're a little screwed up, huh?"

I laugh. "A little but that's okay. We make each other better. Because I know for sure you're what got me through the past six weeks. Reading your messages got me through each day."

"Me too. The first thing I did each morning was check my phone for another message from you."

I grab her hand and lead her back toward the car. "Come for a ride with me?"

"Well, I was supposed to be going on a job but somehow Tara and I got our schedules confused, so she's covering it tonight. I was just going in to the office to catch up on some paperwork. But I'm more than happy to play hooky with you. Where are we going?"

"Back to my place. I want to show you all the changes I made."

Jonah opens the door for us and Rissa slides in first. Once I get in, she plasters herself against my side. I look down at her in amusement. She's feeling as giddy as I am.

When we arrive at my building, we walk through the lobby arm in arm. Rissa grins up at me. "I can't wait to see what you've done. I've missed being here with you."

I know it's hard for her to say it. Insecurity is one of the things we talked about. But after today she'll know that she has nothing to be insecure about. After today she'll know without a shadow of a doubt exactly where she belongs.

I open the door with my key and then let her walk in first. She enters and looks around curiously. Then she stops and looks over her shoulder at me.

"Okay, what's going on?"

I gaze back at her innocently. "What do you mean?"

She gestures around her. "You said you made changes. But it's still completely empty."

I walk over to the kitchen counter. The only furniture I kept was the barstools that sit at this counter. I pick up the wrapped box sitting in one of the seats.

"I did buy something for this place. Something that changes everything." I hand her the box.

She covers her mouth with her hand. "Oh Finn. What did you do?"

"Open the box," I whisper. "Right now."

"Bossy," she mouths. Then she pulls the little bow off and pulls off the top. Inside is a plain black jewelers box. When she looks over at me, I'm watching her closely.

"I *really* hope you don't want me to get down on one knee for this part. Because I might not be able to get back up."

"Finn?" She's half crying, half laughing now. After another exasperated look my way she finally opens the box and then gasps. "Wow."

"Yeah, I might have gone a little overboard but I want everyone who sees you to know the truth."

"What's that?" she asks, her eyes sparkling.

"That you are loved. That you are mine."

She throws herself into my arms and kisses me. *All that physical therapy was definitely worth it*, I think as I carry her back to the bedroom. I set her down gently on the bed and then climb up next to her, tucking her under my arm.

"You never explained why this place is still so empty." She looks at me quizzically.

"When I was deciding what I wanted to change, I realized that there was only one thing I needed to turn this place into a home. And that's you."

She pulls me down for a soft kiss. "You're going to make me cry. That's exactly how I feel. I missed being here so much. But it's not about where we are. I just want to be with you."

"Being with you is all I want, too. As long as you're here, I'm happy. So you can choose to decorate this place however you want."

Her eyes flash right before she breaks out into a huge grin. "I'm going to love decorating this place for you. Think bright colors and tantric sex chairs. This is going to be fun!"

I laugh and it feels so good. I'm healthy, I've got a great family and I've got the love of my life in my arms. I finally feel like I'm exactly where I need to be.

"Welcome home, angel.

The End

You just finished reading the second book in the *BLUE-COLLAR BILLIONAIRES* series. Stay tuned for an excerpt of TANK's book after this.

TANK

is available now!

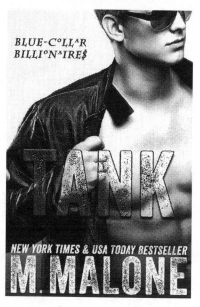

Years ago, Tank Marshall swore off fighting. He exercises iron control to keep his anger in check. But his mother was just diagnosed with cancer and the deadbeat dad he hasn't seen in years is back demanding airtime. Worst of all, a billion dollar inheritance hangs in the balance if he doesn't do what his father wants.

There's only one person that keeps him anchored in the midst of the chaos. One person untouched by violence and money and lies. Emma Shaw. But the one thing that Tank hasn't learned yet is that when billions are at stake, there's no such thing as innocent.

Money. Changes. Everything.

Tank

Darkness hasn't always been my friend. There was a time when I would have been at home asleep in my bed in the middle of the night. Instead I'm prowling the streets, restless and edgy, looking for an outlet for the anger roiling inside.

I glance to my left and right. I'm standing in an alcove that's slightly hidden off the street. It's easier this way. People tend to get nervous if I just hang out. No one stares outright. But there's always a tell. A glance. A step to the side when we pass so our bodies don't touch. Everyone has a "look" about them and mine apparently says *trained killer*.

A group of people spill out of the bar across the street, music and the sound of their voices carrying to where I stand in the shadows. This part of Virginia Beach is a mecca for local college kids looking to blow off steam on the weekends so I rarely have to go looking for trouble.

Trouble usually finds me.

I see the girl first. She has taken her shoes off and is walking barefoot on the concrete. She's beautiful and dressed to score in a short black minidress that shows off long, tanned legs. It doesn't take long for one of the guys in front of the bar to break off from his friends and follow her. I push away from the wall and follow them at a discreet distance. He hooks an arm around her neck. She looks up at him in confusion but grins blearily. He smiles back, with an expression like he just hit the lottery. My blood pressure spikes a notch.

Oh yes. Trouble you miserable bastard, you always find me.

I step out into the road to cross to their side of the street, pulling the hood of my jacket up and over my face.

A horn blares and a taxi screeches to a halt a few inches from me. The driver's side door opens and the cabbie steps out. "What the hell! Look where you're going!"

I glance at him and then back to the couple. Oblivious, they turn down a side street and out of sight. If I wait any longer, I'll lose them. I haven't slept in forty-eight hours and if I don't make sure the girl is all right, then I won't be able to sleep again tonight. Knowing, seeing, is the only thing that gives me some peace. I run across the street, leaving the cab driver gesturing and cursing behind me. By the time I turn the corner, the street is dark. Empty. Then I hear it.

Crying.

He has the girl pressed up against the wall behind a dumpster. She's struggling, pushing at his shoulders while he's working the dress up her legs. He has his other hand over her mouth. Her stiletto shoes are a few feet away from me, abandoned.

That's all it takes for my veins to turn to ice. This is what happens to me right *before*. It's like a red haze that settles over me, blanketing me with the righteous fury necessary to do what needs to be done.

I don't speak; I just yank the guy off her. The first blow stuns him and all the color drains from his face as he doubles over clutching his gut. My mom's words from earlier today ricochet through my mind, shredding my sanity as surely as bullets.

The cancer's back, Tank.

He raises his arm to protect his face or maybe to strike back; I don't know. I hit him with a rib shot, plowing my fists into him over and over. With every connection, I feel stronger.

I need surgery and I don't have the money.

After a while, I don't hear anything. I don't see anything. There's just me, some random dirtbag in an alley and the sensation of fists hitting flesh. All I can do is feel. Hatred. Power.

Purpose.

A whimper pulls me from my adrenaline frenzy. The girl is slumped against the wall, one hand on the grimy stone behind her as she watches me with horror in her eyes. Slowly, I remember where I am. My breath puffs in front of my face, a cloud of white in the frigid night air. The guy is slumped on the ground, his face a bruised, pulpy mass.

I hold out a hand to help her up and she cringes back. My knuckles are scraped and bruised and my hands are covered in blood. I look like something from a horror movie. I put my hands down and move back so she's not crowded.

"It's okay. He can't hurt you anymore."

She nods but continues to regard me with wide, watchful eyes. I'm not sure who she's more afraid of, me or the would-be-rapist bleeding next to the dumpster.

Even more, I'm not sure I want to know.

"Go. Get out of here."

She stumbles to her feet and leans down to grab her shoes. Then she turns back. "What about you? Are you okay?"

"Don't worry about me." She doesn't move, just stands staring at me, her gaze dropping to my bloody hands, so I yell, "Get the hell out of here!"

She runs off this time and doesn't look back. I'm glad because there's nothing she can do for me. I'm beyond saving.

Then I turn back to the man slumped on the ground. "But the rest of you aren't."

* * * * *

By the time I make it back to my car, I can already hear sirens in the distance. The girl probably called the police. They usually do. I've learned not to hang around any longer than necessary. A siren screams past just as I'm driving away.

It takes me about ten minutes to get home. There's an open space right next to my motorcycle so I park and cut the engine. My breath forms white clouds in front of my face. Still I don't move to get out yet. Once I'm inside, I'll be alone with my thoughts again. So

I sit in my car in the empty, dark parking lot, trying not to think about anything. Finally I push the door open and get out.

There's no one to greet me when I enter my apartment. I live alone. No pets and I don't even have any plants that need to be watered. That's always been the way I liked it but things look different lately. My eyes fall on the letter on the counter. It's still in the same place I left it before I went out tonight. I pick it up and read it again. It's another letter from my father's law firm. Another appeal for me to meet his terms. Another offer of money.

My life is a perfect storm lately, a confluence of every thing I fear the most all happening at once.

Two months ago my mom found out that her cancer is back but she just got around to telling me about it today. She told me that she needs surgery. Some rare, expensive surgery that insurance wouldn't cover even if she'd had it. If that wasn't bad enough, there's the sudden reappearance of the father I haven't seen since I was eight. He's supposedly seen the light and wants to establish a relationship with me and my younger brother, Finn. We were both offered huge sums of money if we agree to meet with him regularly. As long as the visits continue, the money will keep coming.

I turned down the first two offers immediately. But now I have a reason to negotiate. The money could help my mom so that's reason enough to consider it. I work for a private security company and my boss has crazy connections. He recommended a lawyer so I've been meeting with him once a week. He's trying to negotiate terms I can live with.

The terms I really want are for him to go back to whatever cave he's been hiding in for the past twenty years. I don't want to see him at all but for my mom, I'm willing to try. There's not much else I can do for her now. I'm helpless and I hate that feeling.

I drop the letter. There's a rust-colored smudge where my finger touched the white stationery. Blood. I hold up my hands, inspecting the damage. I cleaned the worst of it off with a wet wipe in my car but my hands are still filthy. I walk into my room and strip, dropping everything into a pile in the corner. I walk into the bathroom and turn on the water.

I step into the shower. Water rushes over me and then swirls in a dirty red-tinged pool around my feet. Thoughts of what I'm washing off threaten so I grab the bar of soap on the ledge and rub it all over.

The air in the bathroom is cold, sending a chill over my skin. I wrap the towel around my waist and then rub my hair with another one. I'm clean finally. Although I know the feeling won't last. I can wash the outside but there's nothing I can do for how I feel on the inside.

Some stains are permanent.

At least tomorrow I get to see her again. Everyone hates Mondays but lately they're all that's getting me through each week. Sleep, then I can see her. I comfort myself with the thought.

Tomorrow. Just get to tomorrow.

Emma

I race around my room trying to figure out what I'm going to wear. I'm never a fashion plate but especially when I haven't done laundry. The only clean clothes appear to be the ones I wear to wait tables at my second job. Nothing I wear there is appropriate for daylight hours. I toss aside a miniskirt and a glittery top. I need to find something respectable to wear in the next five minutes.

Rummaging through my closet produces a black skirt that's only marginally creased and a striped button down shirt that I never wear because it's too tight. A glance in the mirror on the back of the closet door proves what I already suspect to be true. I look like I've been digging around in trash bins for discarded clothes.

People are going to put change into my coffee cup if I go out looking like this.

I open the door and collide with my sister, Ivy. "Morning. Can I borrow something to wear?"

She eyes my striped shirt and then nods her head. "If that's your alternative, then yes. Hold on."

I follow her to her room but she holds up a hand. "Wait. I'm not alone. Jon stayed the night."

Great. It's a struggle to keep the annoyance off my face. Jon is a lawyer. We met him when he came to the law office where Ivy and I work on behalf of his client, Mr. Marshall.

How did I not hear them come in last night? I must have been dead to the world. Working two jobs has finally caught up with me. But if I'd known that he would be here, I would have gotten up early and left before now. Tired is better than annoyed and disgusted. I can't say any of this to Ivy so I just settle for "Okay."

The door to her room opens and Jon steps into the hall. His dark hair is rumpled and he's got about three days' worth of stubble going on. Ivy gazes up at him and if this were a cartoon, I'm sure there would be little animated stars dancing in her eyes.

"Morning baby." She leans up to give him a kiss. He returns the caress, one hand snaking down to curve around her waist. As he does it, he holds my gaze the entire time.

I contemplate barfing right then and there.

"Never mind. I'll just wear this. You're still covering for me this morning right? I have my financial aid meeting at school."

Ivy gives an exaggerated sigh. "I'll be there. Calm down. I sincerely doubt Patrick cares who is up front answering phones as long as someone is there to do it."

Ivy and I both work for Patrick Stevens, an old friend of the family. I work the front desk while she helps him part-time with bookkeeping and other administrative tasks. After our parents died, he was the one who helped us settle the estate. I'm not sure what we would have done without his help.

Actually I do know. We probably would have lost the house. After all the creditors were tallied and the life insurance was paid, there was nothing left. We were lucky to be able to stay in the house we grew up in at all.

I don't agree with her assumption that he won't care who's up front but I don't have time to argue. The finance office at the local college only accepts appointments at certain times. A year ago, I was in school studying biology. I was planning to go to veterinary school after I finished my undergraduate degree. After our parents were killed, I was too unfocused to continue. Tears still threaten when I think about that day. I blow out a breath and push the ugly memories away.

I had to drop out but I'm finally ready to go back. I've been waiting for weeks to find out whether I've been approved for financial aid for the next school year. I can't miss this meeting.

"Great. Thanks. I'll come straight there when I'm done. I wanted to go check on Mr. Marshall but it can wait."

She makes a face. "Better you than me. I don't have the patience to sit around talking about nothing. That's all old people want to do. I don't know how you do it."

"Maybe she's hoping to be wife number five." Jon smirks when he sees my confused look. "Hell, you're not much younger than the last one."

I have to physically hold myself back from rolling my eyes. He is so sleazy. It's a mystery to me how that sweet old man deals with Jon's slick persona. Then again, he must be used to dealing with arrogant spoiled men.

My face heats thinking about Tank Marshall. He is exactly the kind of guy that I've always avoided. Tall and muscled with the smug aloofness of the naturally beautiful. He's got that same "I'm the center of the universe" arrogance going on that Jon does. It's a shame that one of the first men I feel raw physical chemistry with is exactly the kind of guy I need to stay far away from. I've seen violence, real violence, before so there is nothing about a *bad boy* that I find appealing.

Ivy claps her hands. "It's gross but that would be awesome. Marry the billionaire Em and all our problems are over."

"It's not like that between us. He's a nice old man. We're friends." Not that Ivy would understand the idea of being friends with a man. Sometimes I think my sister only sees two things when she looks at a guy: his dick and his wallet. Friendship is a foreign concept.

She scoffs. "Only you would consider an old geezer your BFF."

I tuck my shirt into my skirt and hustle into the kitchen. I need coffee and something to eat. I have two pieces of bread in the toaster and the coffee percolating when Jon appears in the doorway to the kitchen. I suppress a groan. I see him at work and now he's invading my home.

It feels like I can't escape him sometimes.

"Why didn't you tell me you needed money for school, Emma? I'm sure we can work something out." His eyes roam over my bare legs. It disgusts me that he does this, sometimes right in front of Ivy.

The thing is, he's not even attracted to me.

My sister is *gorgeous*. She's got dark wavy hair and big dramatic brown eyes. I have wispy blond hair and plain gray eyes. She's all smoldering screen siren while I look like the plain country mouse next to her. He's not hitting on me because he's overcome with lust. He's doing it because he's a pig. I've tried to tell Ivy but she doesn't want to hear it. She thinks that he's just flirtatious and doesn't mean anything by it. Love is blind and all that, I guess.

"I've got some loans lined up. I'll be fine."

He leans against the counter and I have to stop so I don't bump into him. He's wearing pajama bottoms but no shirt. If I want my coffee, he's going to make me press up against him to get it.

Not happening.

"Forget it. I'll get coffee on the way." I grab my bag and run out of the house. Ivy calls out to me as the door closes but I don't turn around. There's only so much you can do when someone doesn't want to see the truth.

* * * * *

I smooth my black skirt over my knees and try not to fidget. Across the desk, Mr. Christopher Higgans holds my academic future in his hands. He's been working with me for the past few months to make sure that I can start school again in the fall with a full schedule. I've been applying for every grant that I can for the following school year so that I can finish my bachelor's degree. Loans are always available but I don't want to graduate with a huge cloud of debt hanging over me. I'm hoping that I'm eligible for some scholarships or something.

"Miss Shaw, I've been over your application. There are quite a few loans that we can set up for you. Also you qualify for the Pell

Grant."

I lean forward to review the documents he's pushed across the desk toward me. The numbers are far lower than what I was hoping for.

"So, this is all I can get?"

"This is a great package. The Pell Grant doesn't have to be repaid."

"But the rest of it does? That's a lot of debt."

I'll only be able to take a full semester of classes if I stop working at the law office. My parents left money for me to use for college but I've worked so hard not to touch it. But if I go to school full-time, even with the loans, I'll need to use some of that money to live on. I had considered taking some weekend classes but if I can only do one or two classes a semester, it'll take me forever to finish. I really hate the idea of touching my emergency fund. Once it's gone, I'll have nothing to fall back on.

"Well, yes. But student loans are deferred. You don't have to repay them until you're finished with school. You should be able to start next year with a full semester of classes. And don't forget that you applied for a few grants that will be awarded soon. The committees will notify you directly if you are selected." He's smiling broadly so I can't do anything except smile back and shake his hand before I leave.

The campus of Southern Virginia Community College is a nice place for a walk on a crisp spring day. My sweater doesn't provide much protection from the biting wind but the sun is warm on my face and the breeze is fresh. My parents were so proud that Ivy and I both went to college. My mom finished her degree but my father was a metalworker at the shipyard.

He'd been obsessed with the idea of his daughters getting a college education and I don't think he took a deep breath until the day I moved into the dorms here. Due to Ivy's wild behavior in high school, I think both my parents considered it a minor miracle that neither of their daughters ended up addicted to anything or pregnant before graduation.

Would he have done things differently if he'd known what was coming for him, I wonder? The thought of *that day* hits me in the chest and I halt right in the middle of the pavilion. Instantly I'm back there, in my room, my mom pushing me into the closet and telling me to call for help.

I suck in several deep breaths, feeling lost in the middle of the students who pass me talking excitedly about classes, friends and what they did over the weekend. They pass me by and have no idea that I'm stuck in my personal hell. With the sounds of gunshots ringing in my ears and my mother's screams outside the door.

My bag falls off my shoulder and I let it drop to the ground. I learned how to control the panic attacks in therapy. I focus on the rhythm of my breath, the beat of my heart and the ground below me. I breathe in and hold it for a count of three, then let it out. The artificial breathing pattern slows the rate of my heart and the sense of panic recedes a little. Finally I look around, suddenly aware that I'm standing in the middle of the courtyard gasping for breath.

I pick up my backpack and force myself to start walking. I'm just starting to get my life back on track so I can't allow myself to go back there. Maybe I'm being foolish to think that I'm ready to come back but it's a fallacy that I need to get me through each day. Next year, I'll be in class all day and doing homework all night. I'll need to be focused.

That day has already stolen everything from me. If let it, it'll steal any hope I have for the future. I can't allow that to happen. I don't want to look back on my life and think of all the things I didn't do and never had. That's why I'm so determined to go back and finish my degree. One and a half semesters and I'll be done with my undergraduate degree. Then I can apply to veterinary school. Now all I need to do is figure out where to get the money for all this schooling.

I tilt my face up into the wind and make a promise. *Almost there, Dad.* I'll get back here and finish what I started.

No matter what I have to do.

** *TANK* is available now!

THE ALEXANDERS

~ EBOOKS AVAILABLE ~

BLUE-COLLAR BILLIONAIRES

~ EBOOKS AVAILABLE ~

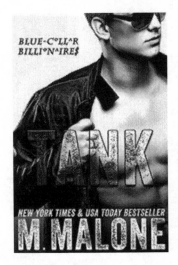

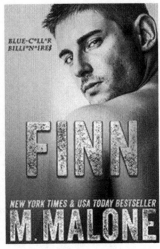

~ COMING SOON ~

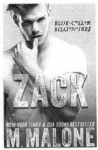

PRINT BOOKS AVAILABLE

THE ALEXANDERS

Book 1 - *One More Day* ~ Jackson + Ridley
(contains Book 0.5 - *Teasing Trent: the prequel*)

Book 2 - *The Things I Do for You* ~ Nick + Raina

Book 3 - *He's the Man* ~ Matt + Penny

Book 4 - *All I Need is You* ~ Eli + Kay
(contains Book 3.5 - *Christmas with The Alexanders*)

Book 5 - *Say You Will* ~ Trent + Mara

BLUE-COLLAR BILLIONAIRES

Book 1 - TANK
Book 2 - FINN

coming soon
Book 3 – GABE
Book 4 – ZACK
Book 4 - LUKE

ABOUT THE AUTHOR

New York Times & USA TODAY Bestselling author M. Malone lives in the Washington, D.C. metro area with her three favorite guys: her husband and their two sons. She likes dramatic opera music, staid old men wearing suspenders, claw-foot bathtubs, and unexpected surprises.

The thing she likes best is getting to make up stuff for a living.

www.MMaloneBooks.com

15204341R00148

Made in the USA
Lexington, KY
12 November 2018